AONARAN:AUTUMN IN THE RAINY SEASON

LAKASH SHARMA

This book is dedicated to all the Introverts and shy people out there in the world, also to those extroverts friends around them who work very hard to change their personalities from Introvert to near Ambivert.

Contents

Contents

Contents

Foreword

Life's most profound moments often occur in the quietest of spaces—over a shared cup of coffee, in the stillness of a late afternoon, or within the unspoken understanding between friends. Aonaran: Autumn in the Rainy Season invites readers into such a space, offering a reflective journey through the intricacies of human connections and the subtle beauty of life's transitions.

Set against the backdrop of a quaint coffee shop, this novel weaves together the lives of two individuals who, through their conversations, reveal the deep layers of their personalities and the complexities of their relationship. It is in this unassuming setting that the story unfolds, presenting a series of encounters that are as gentle as the autumn rain yet as powerful as the emotions they evoke.

The reserved writer at the heart of this tale serves as our guide, leading us through the nuanced terrain of friendship, change, and self-discovery. His dynamic friend, a figure of strength and vulnerability, complements this journey, bringing out the contrasts and harmonies that define their bond. Each chapter, a carefully crafted vignette, captures a moment of realization, a shift in perspective, or a poignant exchange that leaves an indelible mark on both the characters and the readers.

Aonaran: Autumn in the Rainy Season is more than just a story—it is a meditation on the impermanence of life and the enduring power of relationships. It reminds us that in the midst of change, there is beauty to be found, and in the quiet corners of our lives, there is always room for growth and understanding.

As you turn the pages of this novel, allow yourself to be drawn into its contemplative atmosphere. Let the dialogue between the characters resonate with your own experiences, and may the serenity of their world offer you a moment of reflection in your own. Whether you are here for the gentle rhythms of a friendship unfolding or the deeper insights into the human condition, this book is a reminder that even in the smallest moments, there is significance and grace.

Enjoy this journey through autumn's rains and the quiet conversations that define it.

Preface

Aonaran: Autumn in the Rainy Season is a reflective and emotionally rich novel that delves into the nuances of human connections, personal growth, and the serene beauty found within life's transitions. Set predominantly in a cozy coffee shop, the book captures a series of poignant moments shared between a reserved writer and his close friend. Through their dialogues and interactions, the novel explores themes of change, friendship, and self-discovery, providing readers with a deeply engaging and contemplative experience.

The novel unfolds around the protagonist, an introspective writer who frequently visits a charming coffee shop that becomes the backdrop for his evolving relationship with a dynamic friend. Over the course of two months, their meetings become a ritual where they discuss life's complexities, share their aspirations, and support each other through personal struggles.

Each chapter of the book is centered around a significant conversation or event that encapsulates the essence of their friendship and the changes they face. From discussing the symbolism of a peaceful sunset to reflecting on the power of a waterfall, their interactions reveal a deep and evolving understanding of themselves and each other. The narrative weaves these conversations into a broader exploration of life's impermanence and the strength found in relationships.

Acknowledgements

I would like to extend my deepest gratitude to a very special friend who has been a steadfast source of support and encouragement throughout this journey. Her unwavering presence and encouragement have meant the world to me. During the quiet moments when self-doubt crept in and the solitude of writing felt overwhelming, your friendship was a beacon of light.

Your belief in my work and your readiness to listen, offer advice, and share in the highs and lows of this process have been invaluable. This book is as much a testament to your steadfast support as it is to my own efforts. Thank you for being there through it all, and for making the solitary path of writing a little less lonely.

With heartfelt appreciation.

Prologue

Transition from Aonaran: Summer; Season of Societal Flames to Aonaran: Autumn in the Rainy Season

Introduction to the Transition: The transition from Summer: Season of Societal Flames to Aonaran: Autumn in the Rainy Season marks a profound shift in narrative tone and thematic focus. Where the intense heat of Summer explored the raw anguish fueled by societal pressures and personal turmoil, the upcoming season of Autumn in the Rainy Season delves into the reflective and serene aspects of life's transitions. The shift symbolizes a move from fiery adversity to a more contemplative and introspective exploration of change and connection.

From the Scorching Heat to a Refreshing Rain: In Summer: Season of Societal Flames, readers are immersed in a world where the relentless heat represents the intense personal and societal struggles faced by the protagonists. The fire serves as both a literal and metaphorical force that exposes vulnerabilities and challenges the characters to confront harsh truths. As Summer reaches its peak, the flames force the characters into a crucible of self-examination and transformation.

As the oppressive heat of Summer begins to wane, the narrative transitions into the cooling embrace of the rainy season. This shift is not merely a change in weather but a symbolic movement towards a period of reflection and renewal. The scorching flames give way to the gentle, yet persistent, rain of Autumn—a season known for its capacity to cleanse, refresh, and foster new growth.

Entering Autumn in the Rainy Season: In Aonaran: Autumn in the Rainy Season, the setting transitions from the fiery landscape of Summer to the calm and introspective atmosphere of a rainy Autumn. This new season reflects a period of quieter introspection and emotional healing. The protagonist, now grappling with the aftermath of the intense societal flames, finds solace in a serene coffee shop where he frequently meets his close friend.

This Autumn is not characterized by the exuberance of new beginnings alone but by the profound moments of introspection and acceptance brought on by the rain. The gentle showers become a metaphor for the cleansing of past wounds and the renewal of the self amidst the backdrop of life's continuous changes.

Thematic Exploration in the New Season:

From Intensity to Reflection: The transition from Summer's intense fire to the reflective rain of Autumn highlights the shift from confronting harsh societal pressures to exploring internal landscapes. The narrative focuses on finding peace and meaning in the quieter, more personal moments.

Symbolism of Rain and Renewal: Rain in this context symbolizes both the end of tumultuous periods and the beginning of a more introspective phase. It represents the washing away of the old and the nurturing of new growth, mirroring the protagonist's journey towards self-discovery and emotional renewal.

Continuity of Themes: While the setting and tone shift, the themes of empathy, connection, and resilience remain central. The protagonist's interactions with his friend continue to highlight the significance of these elements, even as the external circumstances change.

CHAPTER ONE

JULY

1stJuly

Loyalty is everything

"Why is loyalty everything?" I asked, drawn by the intensity of her conviction.

She paused, her eyes reflecting a mix of determination and vulnerability. "Loyalty is the thread that weaves trust into the fabric of our connections," she replied softly, her voice carrying a weight of experience.

I leaned in, eager to understand her perspective. "It sounds like loyalty holds a deep significance for you," I remarked, sensing there was a story behind her words.

She nodded, her gaze meeting mine with unwavering sincerity. "For me, loyalty is about unwavering support, especially when times are tough."

I listened intently, captivated by her explanation. "In a world where relationships can be fleeting, loyalty becomes a beacon of stability," I mused, trying to grasp the depth of her belief.

She nodded again, a faint smile touching her lips. "It's about standing by each other through thick and thin, knowing someone has your back no matter what."

Her words resonated deeply with me. "So, loyalty is the foundation upon which trust and lasting connections are built," I reflected, realizing the profound truth in her words.

She nodded in agreement, her expression softening with understanding. "Exactly. Loyalty is everything—it's the anchor that holds us steady amidst life's uncertainties."

2ndJuly

You hate the Rain?

"Why do you hate the rain so much?" I asked, curious about the intensity of her disdain.

She sighed, looking out at the dreary landscape through the rain-streaked window. "It just... gets to me, you know? Each drop feels like a tear from the sky, falling without end."

I nodded, trying to understand. "It's more than just the weather for you, isn't it?"

She nodded slowly, her expression distant. "It's like... every raindrop reminds me of all the things that haven't gone right. The missed chances, the disappointments... It's like the universe is crying alongside me."

I watched as she traced a raindrop's path with her finger on the glass. "But rain is also cleansing, isn't it?" I ventured. "Washing away the old, making way for something new."

She smiled faintly, a hint of gratitude in her eyes. "Maybe you're right. Maybe I need to see it differently."

"Sometimes," I continued gently, "we need the rain to appreciate the sunshine. It's a reminder that life has its seasons, its ups and downs."

She nodded again, quieter this time. "I guess I've just been stuck in this rainy season for too long."

"Rain doesn't last forever," I assured her. "It's temporary. And after it passes, there's always a freshness in the air, a sense of renewal."

As we sat in silence, listening to the steady drumming of raindrops, I saw a glimmer of hope in her eyes. Perhaps, in embracing the rain, she could find a way to heal the unseen sorrows within her heart.

"It's just rain," she finally murmured, more to herself than to me. "It can't drown out my spirit forever."

And in that moment, I knew that she was beginning to see the rain not as an enemy, but as a companion on her journey toward brighter skies.

3rdJuly

Happiness on her face.

After a long time, I saw and the sight of her laughter was a revelation, a rare glimpse of joy that seemed to defy the weight of years past.

A rush of emotions stirred within her. It wasn't just happiness that adorned her face; it was a profound sense of relief.

Her cheeks, once often marked with the shadows of distress, now swelled with the vibrancy of her smile. The corners of her eyes crinkled in merriment, reflecting the newfound lightness in her soul.

It was as if the Autumn winds had swept away the remnants of a harsh summer, leaving behind a canvas refreshed and radiant.

I couldn't help but marvel at the transformation.

The face that had once been a map of struggles and hardships was now illuminated by the glow of genuine happiness.

In her laughter, there was a healing power,-

A Promise that the wounds of the past were slowly but surely fading.

4thJuly

Efforts without want

"Sometimes," she said thoughtfully, "efforts without want can be the most meaningful."

I leaned in, curious about her perspective on this intriguing notion. It seemed counterintuitive in a world where desires often drive actions, but her words held a depth that invited deeper exploration.

"For me," she explained, "it's about the purity of intention. Doing something not because I expect a reward or recognition, but simply because it feels right."

Her words resonated with me, prompting memories of times when I had been driven by external motivations rather than intrinsic satisfaction.

"Efforts without want," she continued, "are like planting seeds without knowing if they'll bloom. It's about trusting the process, believing that the act itself holds value regardless of the outcome."

I nodded, beginning to grasp her perspective. There was a humility in her approach, a recognition that true fulfillment often lies in the journey rather than the destination.

She shared stories of people whose selfless efforts had left a lasting impact—the volunteer who quietly served without seeking applause, the artist who created for the joy of creation alone. Each narrative illuminated the beauty of efforts fueled by genuine passion and purpose.

"In a world that often measures success by external validation," she reflected, "efforts without want remind us of our humanity. They reconnect us with the intrinsic joy of giving, creating, and simply being."

As she spoke, I considered moments in my own life where I had experienced this phenomenon—times when I had poured my heart into something not for personal gain but for the sheer love of it.

"Efforts without want," she concluded with a smile, "are a testament to our capacity for selflessness and empathy. They remind us that true fulfillment springs from within, from aligning our actions with our values and convictions."

5thJuly

Unplanned can be beautiful.

"Why can unplanned be beautiful?" I asked, curious about the sentiment behind her words.

She smiled gently, her eyes reflecting a hint of nostalgia. "Because spontaneity brings a sense of adventure and authenticity," she replied, her voice tinged with warmth.

Intrigued, I leaned forward, eager to hear more. "It seems like you've experienced the beauty of the unexpected," I remarked, sensing there was a story waiting to unfold.

She nodded, her gaze thoughtful yet spirited. "Absolutely. Sometimes, the best moments in life happen when we least expect them."

I listened intently, captivated by her perspective. "In a world filled with plans and schedules, spontaneity offers a refreshing change," I reflected, trying to capture the essence of her belief.

She smiled again, a twinkle in her eye. "It's about embracing the unknown, embracing the surprises that life brings."

Her words resonated deeply with me. "So, the unplanned moments hold a special charm, revealing life's spontaneity and joy," I mused, appreciating the beauty in her viewpoint.

She nodded in agreement, her expression serene with contentment. "Exactly. The unplanned can be beautiful—it's a reminder that life is full of delightful surprises waiting to be discovered."

As we savored this conversation, I felt a renewed sense of wonder
for the unexpected treasures that unfold in the spontaneity of life.

6thJuly

Calmness of Water

We sat by the tranquil lake, surrounded by the stillness of nature. The water stretched out before us, reflecting the soft hues of the setting sun. It was in this serene moment that she began to speak of the calmness of water with a serene smile, her eyes reflecting the tranquility she found in its gentle ebb and flow.

"Water has this incredible ability to mirror our inner state," she began, her voice carrying a soothing cadence. "When I look at calm water, I see a reflection of peace and clarity."

Intrigued, I leaned in, captivated by her deep connection to this natural element. "It's like a mirror," I ventured, "showing us our own serenity when we take the time to pause and observe."

She nodded thoughtfully, her gaze drifting to a distant place as if recalling moments spent by serene waters. "Exactly. In a world filled with noise and chaos, water reminds me of the importance of stillness."

Listening intently, I absorbed her perspective. "So, calm water is more than just a sight—it's a metaphor for inner peace and quiet strength," I reflected, trying to capture the essence of her appreciation.

She smiled again, a gentle breeze of understanding passing between us. "Indeed. It teaches us that even amidst turbulence, there's always a place within us where tranquility can be found."

Her words resonated deeply with me. "It's about finding balance," I mused, "and allowing ourselves the space to reflect and restore."

She nodded in agreement, her expression serene with a hint of gratitude. "Yes, the calmness of water invites us to embrace stillness, to listen to the whispers of our own hearts."

As we sat there, enveloped in the quiet rhythm of our conversation, I felt a sense of peace settle within me. The calmness of water, as she described it, was not just a physical attribute but a gentle reminder of the beauty and strength found in quiet moments of reflection.

In her presence, I understood that amidst life's currents, embracing the calmness within could be a source of profound wisdom and resilience.

7thJuly

Nothing goes in my favor

"Nothing seems to go in my favor lately," he sighed, his voice tinged with frustration.

She nodded empathetically, her gaze softening with understanding. "It can feel overwhelming when things don't go as planned," she replied gently.

"I've been trying so hard, but it's like every step forward leads to two steps back," he continued, his shoulders slumping with weariness.

"I know how disheartening that can be," she murmured, her tone compassionate. "But perhaps there's something to learn from these challenges."

He looked at her skeptically, his brow furrowed. "Learn what exactly? That life enjoys throwing obstacles in my path?"

She smiled reassuringly. "Maybe it's about resilience—about finding strength in adversity. Often, our greatest growth comes from navigating through tough times."

He considered her words for a moment, his expression thoughtful. "I suppose you're right," he admitted slowly. "But it's hard to see the silver lining when everything seems to go wrong."

She reached out, placing a comforting hand on his arm. "It's okay to feel frustrated. Sometimes, acknowledging our struggles is the first step towards finding solutions."

"I just wish I could catch a break," he sighed again, his voice tinged with longing.

"Maybe this is a chance to redefine what 'going in your favor' really means," she suggested gently. "Sometimes, it's not about things going perfectly—it's about finding meaning and growth in the journey, no matter how challenging."

He nodded, a flicker of hope crossing his face. "I guess I've been focusing too much on the outcomes," he admitted. "Maybe it's time to embrace the process and trust that things will eventually fall into place."

She smiled warmly, her eyes reflecting encouragement. "Exactly. Life has a way of surprising us when we least expect it. Perhaps this is just a chapter in your story—a chapter that's preparing you for something wonderful."

He nodded again, a newfound determination in his expression. "Thank you," he said sincerely. "I needed that perspective."

8thJuly

Finding Strength Amidst Loss

"Finding Strength Amidst Loss," he sighed, his voice tinged with frustration as they sat together in a quiet corner of the park.

She nodded empathetically, her gaze softening with understanding. "It must have been incredibly tough for you, especially losing someone so dear," she replied gently.

He took a moment, staring at the ground before him, gathering his thoughts. "I was always so introverted," he began quietly. "Never comfortable speaking up, always in my own world. When my grandmother passed away..." His voice caught, and he looked away briefly, struggling to compose himself. "I cried for almost five days straight. It felt like my world had ended. She was the only one who loved me unconditionally, who truly understood me."

"I can't imagine how difficult that must have been," she murmured softly, her tone full of compassion.

"I didn't care about anyone else," he continued, his voice wavering with emotion. "I couldn't bear the thought of living without her guidance, without her love. I felt lost, like everything was meaningless."

"But here you are now," she interjected gently, encouraging him to continue.

He nodded slowly, a tear rolling down his cheek. "Now, I'm learning to live without her. Doing all the things we promised we would do together. It's not easy, but I'm trying."

"It sounds like you've come a long way," she offered warmly, reaching out to place a comforting hand on his arm.

He managed a faint smile, his eyes reflecting a mix of sadness and determination. "So many times in life, it feels like that's it—like everything is over. But we have to wait patiently, like waiting for a bus. Eventually, life lifts us up again and takes us to a new destination."

She nodded in agreement, her expression filled with respect for his journey. "It takes incredible strength to keep going despite the pain. Your grandmother would be proud of how far you've come."

"I hope so," he whispered, his voice filled with quiet resolve. "I miss her every day, but I know she's with me in spirit, guiding me forward."

"Sometimes, our greatest growth comes from the deepest sorrow," she said softly, echoing his earlier sentiments about finding meaning in life's challenges.

He looked at her gratefully, his heart heavy yet somehow lighter from sharing his burden. "Thank you," he said sincerely. "For listening, for understanding."

She smiled warmly, squeezing his hand gently. "You're never alone in your journey. And you've shown incredible courage by embracing life despite your loss."

As they sat together in silence, the park around them seemed to offer a peaceful embrace, a gentle reminder that healing comes with time and with the support of those who care.

9thJuly

Finding peace in Stories.

Her eyes held shadows of sleepless nights, and lines of worry etched upon her brow spoke volumes of the relentless toll on her well-being. Yet, amid her struggle, she found strength to articulate the silent struggles that had shaped her days and haunted her nights.

and into the light of healing.

Her words lingered in the air, heavy with the weight of shared experiences. Across the table, her eyes held mine with a mixture of vulnerability and strength, as if each word she spoke released a burden that had long been carried in silence.

"As I share this with you," she said softly, "I hope you understand what it means to live with these scars."

I nodded, silently acknowledging the courage it took for her to confront her demons and to confide in me. Then, with a gentle resolve, she reached into her bag and placed a book in my hands: "Tuesdays with Morrie." Her fingers lingered on its cover, tracing the title as if it held the key to a sanctuary.I listened intently, the book "Tuesdays with Morrie" still cradled in my hands. It had become more than a gift; it was a lifeline that bridged the gap between her past struggles and the present moment of shared understanding.

"Books have been my lifeline," she continued, her voice steadier now. "In their pages, I find refuge, wisdom, and the resilience to face another day. They anchor me when the world threatens to overwhelm me.""I never imagined I could find such solace in the pages of a book," she confessed, her voice a whisper against the backdrop of the bustling café. "They became my companions when loneliness threatened to consume me, my guides through the labyrinth of pain."

Her words resonated deeply as I held the book—a gift that spoke volumes about her journey. It wasn't just a gesture; it was an invitation into the sanctuary she had found within literature, a place where words breathed life into her weary soul."In literature," she continued, her gaze softening with reminiscence, "I discovered echoes of my own journey, reflections that offered not just solace but a roadmap to healing."

As the afternoon sun filtered through the café windows, casting gentle shadows upon the table between us, I realized that her gift of "Tuesdays with Morrie" was more than a book; it was a testament to the courage to face one's demons and emerge stronger on the other side.

In that moment, I understood the profound impact of her story—a narrative of endurance, of finding solace in the written word amidst the chaos of life's uncertainties. Her vulnerability became a bridge, connecting our shared humanity through the transformative power of storytelling.

As we exchanged a silent nod of mutual understanding, I knew that this chapter of our journey was not just about her story or mine, but about the unspoken bond forged through empathy, resilience, and the beauty of unexpected connections.

10thJuly

Let's laugh together

As the sun gently dipped below the horizon, casting a warm glow over the bustling cafe, I settled into my favorite corner booth with my friend. Laughter, like an old friend, danced around us as we exchanged tales of our day.

"You won't believe what happened at work today," I began, trying to stifle a grin. "I accidentally sent a meme to my boss instead of a report!"

Their eyes widened, and then erupted in laughter. "No way! What did your boss say?"

"He actually replied with a laughing emoji," I chuckled, relieved. "I think he appreciated the humor amidst the chaos."

Moments like these were precious, where the weight of the day melted away in the shared enjoyment of each other's company. It wasn't just the stories themselves that brought laughter but the camaraderie, the understanding that we could find humor even in the mundane.

"You know," they said, wiping tears of laughter from their eyes, "these moments with you remind me why friendship is so important. It's not just about sharing the good times but also finding joy in the little absurdities of life."

I nodded in agreement, savoring the warmth of their words. "Absolutely. Laughter bonds us in a way that nothing else can. It's a reminder to not take ourselves too seriously."

Our evening stretched into the night, the cafe gradually emptying around us. Yet, our spirits remained buoyant, fueled by the endless reservoir of shared laughter. We reminisced about childhood escapades, embarrassing moments that turned into cherished memories, and dreams that seemed ludicrous now but were once our greatest aspirations.

As we finally bid farewell, promising to meet again tomorrow, I couldn't help but reflect on the simple yet profound joy of laughter. In a world often fraught with challenges, it was these moments of levity that anchored us, reminding us of the beauty of friendship and the healing power of laughter.

So, here's to laughter – to the spontaneous giggles, the uncontrollable snorts, and the shared mirth that lightens our hearts. May we always find reasons to laugh together, weaving threads of joy into the tapestry of our lives.

11thJuly

You found the friendship, you never Want to lose

"Guess what happened today?" I began, unable to contain my amusement. "I tried baking a cake from scratch for the first time, and let's just say it ended up looking more like a pancake!"

Their eyes sparkled with mirth, mirroring my own amusement. "Oh no! Did it at least taste good?"

I chuckled, shaking my head. "Not really, but the kitchen definitely smelled like a bakery gone wrong for hours!"

Moments like these, where laughter effortlessly intertwined with our conversations, were what made our friendship priceless. It wasn't just the stories we shared, but the way we could find humor in the everyday mishaps and turn them into memories.

"You know," they said with a grin, "it's moments like this that make me grateful for our friendship. Even the simplest things become special when we're together."

I nodded in agreement, touched by the sincerity in their words. "Absolutely. It's the laughter and the ability to find joy in each other's company that make our bond so strong."

"You know," they said, wiping tears of laughter from their eyes, "these moments with you remind me why friendship is so important. It's not just about sharing the good times but also finding joy in the little absurdities of life."

I nodded in agreement, savoring the warmth of their words. "Absolutely. Laughter bonds us in a way that nothing else can. It's a reminder to not take ourselves too seriously."

There's a comfort in knowing that no matter what happens, your friend understands you at your core. Conversations flow effortlessly, laden with shared jokes, unspoken understandings, and a depth of empathy that goes beyond words. It's as if their joys are your joys, their sorrows your sorrows—a seamless blending of emotions that heightens the highs and softens the lows.

In this friendship, apologies are swift and sincere, ego bends without breaking, and forgiveness is innate. There's no need for pride or resentment because vulnerability is met with compassion, and mistakes are embraced as opportunities for growth together.

Time spent with such a friend is not just leisurely—it's essential. It nourishes the soul, fuels creativity, and provides a safe space to explore thoughts and feelings without fear of judgment. Whether it's a late-night conversation or a spontaneous adventure, every moment is infused with a sense of belonging and acceptance.

The bond is forged through shared experiences—laughter that echoes through empty streets, tears shed in moments of vulnerability, and silent support during life's storms. It's built on a foundation of mutual respect, trust that grows deeper with each passing day, and a willingness to celebrate each other's successes as if they were your own.

In this friendship, differences fade into insignificance because what truly matters is the connection of hearts and minds. It's a bond where silence speaks volumes and presence speaks louder than words—a companionship that defies distance, time, and circumstance.

To have such a friend is a gift beyond measure. They are not just a friend but a mirror reflecting your best self, a confidant who understands your fears and hopes, and a pillar of strength during life's uncertainties.

12thJuly

What do you wanna hear?

"Guess what happened today?" I began, unable to contain my excitement. "I finally mustered up the courage to apply for that dream job I've been eyeing for months!"

Their eyes lit up with genuine happiness for me, echoing my own excitement. "That's amazing! How did it go? Tell me everything!"

I laughed nervously, recounting every detail of the interview, from the challenging questions to the unexpected moments of connection with the interviewer. Their unwavering support and genuine interest made me feel understood and appreciated.

Moments like these, where joy effortlessly intertwined with our conversations, were what made our friendship invaluable. It wasn't just the achievements we celebrated together, but the way we shared in each other's aspirations and victories.

"You know," they said with a smile, "it's moments like this that remind me how lucky I am to have you as a friend. Your successes feel like my own."

I nodded in agreement, touched by their heartfelt words. "Absolutely. It means so much to have someone who genuinely cheers for you and shares in your excitement."

"You know," they continued, "these moments with you make me realize the true beauty of friendship. It's not just about being there during tough times but also celebrating every little triumph, big or small."

I smiled warmly, grateful for their unwavering support. "Indeed. Having someone who celebrates with you makes the journey so much sweeter."

There's a comfort in knowing that no matter what happens, your friend is there to lift you up. Conversations flow effortlessly, filled with shared dreams, unspoken encouragement, and a depth of understanding that strengthens the bond.

In this friendship, support is unconditional, advice is given with love, and encouragement is ever-present. There's no room for envy or competition because your friend's success is your joy, and your victories are their source of pride—a harmonious exchange of positivity that amplifies both highs and lows.

Time spent with such a friend is not just enjoyable—it's essential. It nurtures confidence, fuels ambition, and provides a safe space to dream and achieve without fear of judgment. Whether it's late-night brainstorming sessions or spontaneous celebrations, every moment is infused with a sense of mutual respect and empowerment.

The bond is forged through shared dreams—laughter that echoes through jubilant moments, tears shed in times of vulnerability, and unwavering support during life's challenges. It's built on a foundation of trust, a belief in each other's potential, and a commitment to seeing dreams realized together.

In this friendship, differences are celebrated because what truly matters is the connection of hearts and the shared journey of growth. It's a bond where silence speaks volumes and presence speaks louder than words—a companionship that transcends distance, time, and circumstance.

To have such a friend is a treasure beyond measure. They are not just a companion but a cheerleader who celebrates your victories as passionately as their own, a confidant who understands your aspirations and fears, and a steadfast ally who believes in you, even when you doubt yourself.

13thJuly

Sunset

As the sun dipped low on the horizon, casting hues of orange and pink across the rippling surface of the river, we sat in companionable silence, each lost in our own thoughts. It was one of those evenings where words seemed unnecessary, where the beauty of the sunset spoke volumes on its own.

"Isn't it breathtaking?" I finally murmured, breaking the silence as I glanced over at my friend.

She nodded slowly, her gaze fixed on the shifting colors of the sky. "Absolutely. Sunsets always remind me of the beauty in endings and the promise of new beginnings."

I smiled, touched by her insight. "It's like each sunset is a reminder that even when things seem to be coming to a close, there's always hope for another day."

We sat there, silently soaking in the serenity of the moment, feeling the gentle breeze caress our faces as the sky continued its transformation from vibrant hues to dusky shades. The river mirrored the sky's canvas, creating a scene that felt both surreal and comforting.

"You know," she said softly, her voice barely above a whisper, "moments like this make me appreciate the simplicity of just being here, sharing this experience with you."

I nodded, a lump forming in my throat at the sincerity in her words. "Likewise. It's moments like these that make me realize how fortunate I am to have a friend like you."

In the fading light, we reminisced about similar evenings spent by the riverbank, sharing dreams and fears, laughter and tears. It was in these quiet moments that our bond felt strongest, anchored not just in shared experiences but in a mutual understanding of life's ebbs and flows.

"There's something comforting about knowing that no matter where life takes us," she said softly, "we can always find solace in moments like this."

I nodded in agreement, grateful for the warmth of her presence beside me. "Absolutely. It's moments like these that remind me of the beauty in simple connections and the strength they provide."

14thJuly

Still Waiting for her.

As the dawn broke over the city, casting a soft golden light across the rooftops, I found myself once again lost in thoughts of her. The previous evening's sunset had left an indelible impression, its beauty amplified by her presence. The way she spoke about endings and new beginnings lingered in my mind, resonating with the uncertainty of our own friendship.

I recalled how we had sat by the riverbank, enveloped in the tranquil atmosphere, our conversation weaving effortlessly between shared memories and contemplative silence. Her words about appreciating the moment had struck a chord within me, reminding me of the delicate balance between holding onto the present and anticipating the future.

Yet, despite the warmth of our connection, there was an unspoken longing in my heart as I waited for her next message, her next call. The simplicity of our friendship was a refuge, a haven where words often felt unnecessary yet comforting. But now, in the quiet solitude of the morning, I couldn't help but wonder if our bond meant the same to her.

The gentle breeze that had brushed against us by the riverbank seemed distant now, replaced by a sense of anticipation tinged with uncertainty. I yearned for another evening like that, where the sunset painted the sky in hues of promise and where her presence felt like the most natural thing in the world.

And so, as the city stirred awake and life carried on around me, I found myself still waiting for her, hoping that the simplicity of our shared moments would continue to weave our stories together, painting a canvas of friendship that transcended the passing of days.

15thJuly

Surprise went wrong.

As the sun cast its golden hue over the cozy café, I nestled into our favorite booth, the familiar chatter wrapping around us like a warm blanket. My friend, with a curious glint in her eyes, leaned in, ready for our usual exchange of stories.

"I have some exciting news!" I announced, barely containing my enthusiasm. "My first book is set to publish in just a few days!"

Her expression shifted instantly, a mix of surprise and frustration crossing her face. "Wait, what? You're publishing a book? And you didn't tell me?" Her tone was playful, but the underlying annoyance was clear.

I chuckled nervously, trying to diffuse the moment. "I know, I know! I wanted it to be a surprise, but I didn't mean to hide it from you."

"You know I love your writing," she said, arms crossed, but I could see the corners of her mouth twitching. "You articulate things so beautifully, yet here I am, hearing it from the café gossip instead of you!"

We both burst into laughter, the tension melting away like ice in the summer sun. "I promise, it wasn't intentional! I just got caught up in the whirlwind of deadlines."

With a playful roll of her eyes, she finally broke into a smile. "Well, you better bring me a signed copy! And maybe one of those Nescafé frappés you owe me?"

"Deal!" I replied, waving to the barista for our favorite drinks. As we sipped on our frosty treats, we dove into a delightful conversation about the book's journey, sharing dreams, fears, and the joy of creating something meaningful.

Each sip seemed to add a sprinkle of happiness, gradually washing away any remnants of her initial anger. "You know," she mused, her eyes sparkling again, "even though I'm a bit upset, I'm so proud of you. You've worked hard for this!"

"Thanks! It means the world to me to have your support," I grinned back, feeling lighter as we basked in the joy of friendship.

As the evening drew on, the café buzzed softly around us, but we were in our own little world, weaving dreams and laughter together. It was moments like these—filled with unexpected news, a hint of tension, and a whole lot of love—that reminded us of the true essence of our bond.

So here's to surprises, to Nescafé frappés shared over laughter, and to the beautiful chaos of friendship that makes life all the more vibrant!

16thJuly

Excited

She sat eagerly in their favorite corner of the bustling café. She fidgeted with her phone, occasionally glancing up at the door with an excited smile, her anticipation palpable.

Finally, after what felt like an eternity but was actually just a few minutes, the door swung open, and her friend entered with a wide grin spread across her face. She jumped up from her seat, waving enthusiastically. "You're here!"

Her friend rushed over, enveloping her in a tight hug. "I've been looking forward to this all week!" she exclaimed, her voice filled with genuine excitement. "I can't wait for our day together."

They settled back into their booth, drinks in hand, the familiar chatter of the café blending into the background as they caught up on life. She couldn't help but notice how her friend's eyes sparkled with happiness, a stark contrast to the weariness she had seen in them before.

"You know," her friend began, her voice soft but earnest, "you've been my rock through everything. When I was struggling with societal expectations and norms, feeling like I didn't belong, you were always there to remind me of my worth."

She smiled warmly, touched by her friend's words. "You've always had the strength within you," she replied. "I just helped you see it."

Her friend nodded, a grateful expression on her face. "You gave me the courage to stand up for myself, to live authentically despite the challenges. Today, I feel free."

As they shared stories and laughter throughout the day, she couldn't shake the feeling of relief and happiness that washed over her. Seeing her friend genuinely happy and at peace was a balm to her soul, knowing the struggles she had faced.

As the evening approached, they reluctantly prepared to part ways. Her friend hugged her tightly once more, gratitude and joy evident in every gesture. "Thank you for today," her friend whispered. "I needed this."

She hugged her friend back, feeling a sense of fulfillment. "Anytime," she replied softly. "I'm always here for you."

With a final wave, her friend left the café, her steps lighter than when she had arrived. She watched her go, a sense of pride swelling within her. Despite the heaviness of her friend's struggles, today had been a reminder that genuine moments of happiness and connection could lighten even the heaviest burdens.

17thJuly

Letting Go.

She and her friend found themselves immersed in a deep conversation about the complexities of relationships and the art of letting go.

"It's just frustrating, you know?" she sighed, stirring her coffee absentmindedly. "I always put in so much effort into friendships and relationships, but it feels like no one really cares about that."

Her friend nodded sympathetically, her expression softening with understanding. "I get it. It's hard when you feel like you're the only one invested in making things work."

"Yeah," she continued, a hint of frustration in her voice. "I've come to realize that we can't force people to value us or appreciate our efforts. If someone isn't happy with me or doesn't feel the same way about our friendship, why should I keep trying to please them?"

Her friend leaned in, listening intently. "You're right. We can't control how others feel or what they want. Sometimes, letting go is the healthiest choice, even though it's difficult."

She nodded, a sense of resolve growing within her. "Exactly. I've reached a point where I'm tired of trying to hold on to relationships that drain me. Those who want to be a part of my life will stay because they genuinely want to, not because I'm begging them to."

Her friend smiled gently, sensing her determination. "You deserve friendships and relationships where you're valued and appreciated for who you are. It's okay to prioritize your own happiness and well-being."

Taking a deep breath, she felt a weight lifting off her shoulders. "Absolutely. I'm done wasting my energy on those who don't deserve it. From now on, I'm focusing on nurturing the connections that bring positivity and joy into my life."

As they sipped their coffee in companionable silence, she felt a sense of clarity and empowerment. The conversation had been a cathartic release, reaffirming her decision to let go of toxic dynamics and embrace those who genuinely cared about her.

"We spend so much time and effort trying to please everyone," she reflected quietly. "But in the end, what matters most is our own happiness and peace of mind."

Her friend nodded in agreement, a shared understanding passing between them. "You're taking a brave step towards prioritizing yourself," she said warmly. "And I'm here to support you every step of the way."

18thJuly

Healing

"You know, these past few months have been the hardest of my life," she began, her voice carrying a mixture of vulnerability and strength.

Her friend nodded gently, their eyes full of empathy. "I can't even imagine what you've been through. It must have been incredibly tough."

She looked down at her tea, stirring it slowly. "It was. There were days when I didn't think I could get through it. Everything felt like it was falling apart."

"I'm so sorry you had to go through that," her friend said softly, reaching out to squeeze her hand in reassurance.

Taking a moment to collect her thoughts, she continued, "But you know what's strange? As painful as it was, it also taught me so much about myself and about resilience."

Her friend smiled warmly. "That's a powerful insight. Sometimes, our darkest moments become catalysts for growth."

She nodded, a small smile tugging at her lips. "Exactly. I've been learning to give myself permission to feel everything—to grieve, to be angry, to be hopeful. It's all part of the healing process."

"I'm glad you're allowing yourself that space," her friend replied, their gaze unwaveringly supportive.

"Yeah," she continued, a thoughtful look crossing her face. "I've been focusing a lot on self-care too—doing things that make me feel grounded and whole again. It's amazing how much a simple walk in nature or writing in my journal can help."

"It sounds like you're really nurturing yourself," her friend remarked, admiration evident in their voice.

She nodded gratefully. "I am. And I'm starting to see glimpses of light at the end of this tunnel. I know I'll come out of this stronger."

Her friend leaned forward, their expression earnest. "You already are. It takes immense strength to face what you've faced and to keep moving forward."

Their eyes met in a moment of shared understanding, the unspoken bond between them a source of comfort.

"You've been such a huge part of my healing journey," she said sincerely. "Just having you listen and support me has meant more than words can say."

Her friend smiled softly. "I'm honored to be here for you. Always."

19thJuly

Presence of Introverts

She stared out the window, lost in her thoughts, while he sat beside her, a comforting presence in the midst of her sorrow.

"You know," she began softly, "there's something incredibly comforting about your presence during times like this."

He, usually reserved and introspective, glanced at her with a hint of curiosity. "What do you mean?"

"I mean," she continued, turning to face him, "sometimes I just need someone who can sit with me in silence. Someone who understands that I'm not looking for advice or solutions. I just want to feel the weight of my emotions without feeling pressured to 'fix' anything."

A flicker of understanding crossed his expression as he nodded slowly. "Ah, I see. You mean someone who can simply be there with you, without trying to change or analyze the situation."

"Exactly," she replied, a sense of relief washing over her. "Someone who doesn't feel the need to fill the silence with empty words or so-called expert advice that only adds to the noise."

He chuckled softly, a rare smile gracing his features. "I guess being an introvert has its perks then, huh? We're pretty good at being quiet and just being present."

She smiled gratefully. "More than just 'pretty good.' It's invaluable, especially when I'm feeling overwhelmed."

He nodded thoughtfully, his gaze gentle and understanding. "I'm glad I can be that person for you, even if it's just sitting quietly together."

"You have no idea how much it means to me," she confessed, her voice sincere. "To have a friend who respects my need for silence and who doesn't try to fix everything. It's a rare and precious gift."

20thJuly

Past Experiences

"You know," she began tentatively, "I've been thinking a lot about the mistakes I've made in the past."

He nodded, his expression thoughtful. "It's natural to reflect on those things. What's been on your mind?"

She sighed softly, tracing the rim of her coffee cup with her finger. "I guess I've been replaying certain decisions and actions, wondering if I could have handled things differently."

"I think we all do that from time to time," he replied gently. "It's part of growing and learning."

"Yeah," she continued, her voice tinged with regret. "There are moments when I wish I had listened more, or been more patient. Maybe then things wouldn't have turned out the way they did."

He leaned forward, his gaze steady. "It's important to acknowledge those feelings. But remember, we can't change the past. What matters is how we use those lessons moving forward."

She nodded slowly, absorbing his words. "You're right. I've been trying to see these mistakes as opportunities for growth rather than dwelling on them."

"I've also realized," she said after a pause, "that forgiving myself is just as important as learning from my mistakes."

21stJuly

Being Non Serious in Serious World

"You know," I said with a laugh, "sometimes it feels like everyone takes life too seriously."

She nodded, a mischievous glint in her eyes. "I get that. It's like everyone's rushing to solve big problems without stopping to enjoy the little things."

"Exactly!" I exclaimed, waving my hand. "There are important issues, but we forget to laugh and enjoy simple pleasures."

She grinned, agreeing. "We need to remember to take a break and not let everything weigh us down."

"That's where our not-so-serious approach helps," I continued, smiling. "We find joy in silly things, laugh at ourselves, and go on spontaneous adventures."

She chuckled, remembering a recent escapade. "Remember when we skipped work for a road trip to nowhere? Just because we felt like it?"

I laughed too, recalling the memory. "Oh yes! We found a tiny diner in the middle of nowhere and had the best pie ever."

"Exactly," she nodded, eyes sparkling. "Those moments remind me why it's important to stay light-hearted in a serious world."

"I think," I said thoughtfully, "our approach isn't about ignoring problems. It's about finding balance, knowing when to take things lightly and when to dig deep."

"Absolutely," she agreed seriously. "It's about staying sane in a world that can overwhelm us."

22ndJuly

Accepting Someone's Weaknesses

My friend and I enjoyed the peacefulness of the afternoon in the campus of University.

"You know," I began thoughtfully, "I've been thinking about how we often judge people based on their strengths, but sometimes overlook their weaknesses."

She nodded, her expression thoughtful. "That's so true. We tend to admire people for their accomplishments and strengths, but we all have vulnerabilities and struggles that make us human."

"Yeah," I continued, "I've realized that true acceptance and empathy come from understanding someone's weaknesses as much as their strengths. It's about seeing the whole person."

She smiled warmly. "Absolutely. It's in those moments of vulnerability that we connect on a deeper level with others. It's where true empathy and compassion come into play."

I leaned back, gazing at the rippling water. "I think about times when I've felt most accepted and valued—it's when someone sees my flaws and supports me anyway."

"That's when you know someone truly cares," she agreed, nodding in understanding. "When they accept you unconditionally, weaknesses and all."

"And it goes both ways," I reflected. "Learning to accept others in their entirety, not just their strengths, enriches our relationships and builds stronger connections."

~

23rdJuly

It's always You and her Vs the problem, but now the problem is You vs Her

"You know," she began, her voice tinged with a hint of concern, "it's always been 'you and me against the problem.' But lately, it feels like the problem has become 'you versus me.'"

Her words hung in the air, laden with a weight that mirrored the gravity of our conversation. It was a stark realization, one that pierced through the camaraderie and shared experiences that had defined our friendship for years. What began as a dialogue about life's challenges had subtly shifted into a reflection on the complexities and conflicts that can arise between even the closest of friends.

I listened intently, my mind racing to grasp the depth of her sentiment. For so long, we had navigated obstacles together, drawing strength from our unity and mutual support. Whether it was tackling personal dilemmas, navigating professional setbacks, or simply offering a shoulder to lean on during turbulent times, we had always been a formidable team.

But now, as she pointed out, the dynamics had changed. The very essence of our bond seemed to be tested by tensions and disagreements that had surfaced between us. What was once a shared struggle against external challenges had evolved into an internal conflict, where our individual perspectives and desires seemed to clash.

"It's not that I don't value our friendship," she continued, her tone tinged with a hint of vulnerability. "But it's like we're on opposite sides of this issue, and I don't know how to bridge that divide."

Her words struck a chord within me, prompting a flood of memories that underscored the depth of our connection. We had weathered storms together, celebrating triumphs and consoling each other through setbacks. Our friendship had been built on a foundation of trust, understanding, and unwavering support.

And yet, here we were, grappling with a rift that seemed to widen with each passing moment. It was a poignant reminder of the intricacies inherent in any relationship—the delicate balance between harmony and discord, unity and divergence.

As I searched for words to respond, I realized that acknowledging the shift in our dynamic was the first step toward reconciliation. It was a testament to the evolution of our friendship—a recognition that growth sometimes entails confronting challenges head-on, even when they threaten to strain the bonds we hold dear.

"We've faced obstacles before," I ventured, striving to convey reassurance amidst the uncertainty. "And just as we've overcome them in the past, I believe we can find a way through this too."

Her eyes met mine, reflecting a blend of apprehension and hope. In that moment, I knew that while the path forward might not be clear-cut, our shared history and mutual respect would serve as guiding lights in navigating the complexities of our current predicament.

As we lingered over our coffee, our conversation shifted from introspection to a renewed commitment—a pledge to confront our differences with empathy, to seek understanding amidst discord, and to reaffirm that, despite the challenges we faced, our friendship remained a cornerstone of strength and resilience.

24thJuly

Don't be content

In the quiet corner of a cozy café, amidst the gentle hum of conversation and the aroma of freshly brewed coffee, my friend shared a thought that lingered long after our meeting had ended. "Don't be content when people say they love you and care for you," she began, her voice carrying a weight of experience and reflection. "The real question is: until when? Because just like seasons, people change."

Her words resonated deeply, cutting through the veneer of comfort that often accompanies expressions of affection. It was a sentiment both sobering and thought-provoking, challenging the conventional wisdom that love and care are steadfast and enduring.

As we delved deeper into her perspective, it became clear that she wasn't dismissing the significance of hearing such sentiments. Rather, she was urging a deeper examination of their authenticity and longevity. In a world where words can be fleeting and emotions transient, she advocated for a tempered optimism—one that appreciates the present but remains mindful of the uncertainties of the future.

"People change," she reiterated, her eyes reflecting a blend of wisdom and melancholy. It was a reminder that relationships evolve, shaped by time, circumstances, and the complexities of human nature. Just as seasons mark the passage of time with their distinct hues and temperatures, so too do people undergo transformations, sometimes imperceptibly, other times with startling clarity.

Her analogy of seasons was not just poetic; it was a metaphor for the natural ebb and flow of human connections. Like the shifting winds and changing landscapes of each season, our relationships can experience periods of warmth and closeness, followed by moments of distance and change. It's a cycle as old as time itself, a reminder that love is not immune to the passage of years or the shifting tides of life.

Yet, amidst this acknowledgment of impermanence, there lay a glimmer of hope—a call to cherish the moments of genuine connection as they unfold, to savor the beauty of love in its myriad forms, even as we acknowledge its inherent fragility. It's about finding resilience in the face of change, about nurturing relationships with care and understanding, knowing that true love transcends mere words.

As I reflected on her words in the days that followed, I couldn't help but think of the wisdom they held. It's not about succumbing to cynicism or doubt, but rather about embracing a deeper understanding of love—one that honors its complexities and acknowledges its capacity for growth and transformation.

In the end, her message was one of mindfulness and perspective—an invitation to appreciate the depth of affection in our lives while remaining attuned to the winds of change that shape our journey. Just as seasons give way to one another, so too do our relationships evolve, each phase carrying its own lessons and blessings.

25thJuly

Silence

In the quiet corner of their favorite café, a noticeable silence settled between the two friends. The usual buzz of conversation and the aroma of coffee were there, but the atmosphere felt tense and different.

He: "Is everything okay? You seem a bit off today."

She: silence, looking distant

He: "I'm here if you want to talk about anything."

She: sighs "Just... Could you please sit with me? And maybe... just be quiet for a bit? I'm not feeling great."

He: taken aback "Of course, I understand. I'm here."

The silence between them grew, heavy with unspoken thoughts and emotions. It wasn't the usual cheerful banter they shared, but a moment where she needed space and quiet support.

He (thinking): contemplating Silence can be powerful. Sometimes, just being there silently can mean more than any words.

It taught him the importance of being present and supportive, even in moments of silence.

26thJuly

I am OK..

The day after their quiet moment, he approached their usual spot with a mixture of curiosity and concern. Would their friendship resume its usual warmth, or would yesterday's silence cast a lingering shadow?

He: "Hey, how are you feeling today?"

She: smiling softly "I'm sorry about yesterday. I wasn't myself. Thank you for sitting with me."

He: nodding understandingly "No need to apologize. I'm glad you're feeling better."

Their exchange was gentle, marked by an unspoken acknowledgment of the complexities of human emotions. She shared a heartfelt reflection on her state of mind, revealing the internal struggle she faced—a familiar battle between feeling strong and resilient one moment, only to confront uncertainty and doubt the next.

She: "Sometimes, it's like I've conquered everything, and other times, I feel stuck where I began. I was confused yesterday, but now I feel okay. I appreciate your understanding and respecting my need for silence."

Their experience taught him that true friendship isn't just about being there during the good times but also offering support and understanding during moments of uncertainty and introspection.

27thJuly

Craving

He noticed her demeanor—a mixture of contemplation and a subtle yearning that hinted at something deeper beneath the surface.

He: "You seem a bit quieter than usual today. Is everything alright?"

She: Pausing for a moment, she looked into her coffee cup, then met his gaze with a hint of vulnerability. "You know, I've been feeling this strong craving lately. Not for anything material or specific, but for that connection, that feeling of being able to hug someone special."

He listened intently, sensing the weight behind her words. It wasn't just a passing comment; it was a glimpse into her inner world, where emotions and desires intertwined.

She continued, her voice soft but resolute: "I want someone with whom I can share the darkest and lightest experiences, someone who will hear me, listen to me, maybe even correct me sometimes. And yes, someone who will just tightly hug me when words aren't enough. It's like a dream I wish could be fulfilled."

Her confession hung in the air, a poignant admission of her longing for emotional connection and support. He nodded understandingly, knowing that their friendship had always been a safe space for such conversations.

He: "I understand. It's natural to crave that kind of deep connection. To have someone who can be there for you in every way you need."

It wasn't about romantic gestures or grand declarations; it was about the quiet understanding and unwavering support that defined their friendship.

28thJuly

Sorry

She sat across from him, a thoughtful expression on her face, as if grappling with something that had been weighing on her mind.

She: "You know, I've been thinking... I owe you an apology."

He looked at her with a mixture of curiosity and concern, unsure where this was leading.

He: "What for?"

She took a deep breath, her words carefully chosen yet carrying a hint of remorse.

She: "Every time we meet, you always ask about me. And whenever I have a problem or something bothering me, I talk about it, and you listen. But yesterday, after our conversation, I realized something. I've been so caught up in my own world that I never really asked about you. I never gave you the space to talk about your own matters. I feel like I've been selfish, always talking about myself."

Her confession hung in the air, a vulnerable admission of self-awareness and gratitude.

He: "It's okay, really. I've never felt like you were being selfish. You have a lot going on, and I'm glad you feel comfortable sharing with me."

She shook her head gently, a faint smile playing on her lips.

She: "No, it's not just that. I've also realized something else. You always listen to me without any agenda, without trying to one-up my problems with your own. You never talk about your own bad experiences or struggles, even when I know you have them. You just listen, and I appreciate that more than I can express."

Her words resonated deeply with him. It wasn't often that someone acknowledged his role in their life so candidly.

He: "I'm here for you, always. If you need to talk, I'll listen. And don't worry about not asking about me. It's okay. Sometimes, listening is all that's needed."

She carried with her a deeper gratitude for his unwavering presence in her life, while he felt a quiet satisfaction in knowing that their friendship was based on genuine care and empathy.

29thJuly

Pause

He: I've been feeling really tense lately. It's like everything is moving too fast, and I can't catch my breath.

She: (Nods understandingly) Sometimes it feels like life is on fast-forward, right?

He: Exactly. I think I need a pause, you know? A break from everything.

She: You're not alone in feeling that way. It's okay to feel stuck sometimes.

He: But I feel like I should be doing more, achieving more. It's like I'm falling behind.

She: (Sincerely) You don't have to have it all figured out right now. Taking a pause isn't a setback—it's a chance to gather yourself.

He: I just don't know where to start.

She: (Thoughtfully) Start by giving yourself permission to pause. Maybe take a day off, do something you enjoy without pressure.

30thJuly

No Thoughts

She sat across from him in the quiet corner of the cafe, sipping her coffee as she observed her friend, who seemed lost in thought. His usually lively demeanor was replaced by a solemn expression, his gaze distant as if staring through the window at something unseen.

She: "Hey, you seem a bit off today. Is everything okay?"

He looked up, a flicker of uncertainty crossing his face before he sighed, his shoulders slumping slightly.

He: "I... I don't know. I just... I don't have any thoughts."

She furrowed her brow, concern evident in her eyes as she tried to understand what he meant.

She: "No thoughts? What do you mean?"

He struggled to find the words, his voice barely above a whisper as he tried to articulate the weight of his emotions.

He: "I mean... I don't have anything to say. I don't know how to explain it. It's like... I'm lost. I don't even know what's bothering me anymore."

Her heart sank as she realized the depth of his struggle. She had always known him as someone who was quick-witted and articulate, but now he was grappling with a silence that seemed heavier than words could convey.

She: "It's okay. You don't have to explain. I'm here for you, no
matter what."

He looked at her gratefully, appreciating her understanding even
when he couldn't find the words to describe his inner turmoil.

He: "Thank you. I just... I feel stuck, you know? Like I don't even
know what's going on in my own head."

31stJuly

She went

I sat there, savoring a moment of quiet amidst the familiar surroundings, when my phone buzzed softly on the table. Curious, I glanced down to see her name flashing on the screen.

Without hesitation, I answered, expecting the usual cheerful banter that often filled our spontaneous phone calls. Instead, her voice sounded slightly distant, tinged with an unfamiliar edge of hurried explanation.

She: "Hey, I just wanted to let you know... I'm not in town."

Her words hung in the air, a sudden twist in the script of our daily routines. I paused, trying to process the unexpected revelation. Not in town? Why hadn't she mentioned anything before?

Me: "Not in town? Where are you?"

She sighed softly, her tone carrying a mix of apology and explanation.

She: "I had to go to Kashmir for work. It all happened so fast, I didn't get a chance to tell you."

Her words resonated deeply within me. Here I was, comfortably settled into the rhythm of daily life, while she navigated a world beyond our usual shared experiences. It dawned on me that everyone has their own journey, their own obligations that sometimes take them away without warning.

As I sat there, absorbing the reality of her absence, a wave of understanding washed over me. We often assume a sense of entitlement over others' time and attention, forgetting that life unfolds with its own demands and priorities. She hadn't left to neglect our friendship but had simply followed the path her responsibilities laid out before her.

In that moment, I realized the importance of empathy and perspective. We are interconnected yet independent, weaving in and out of each other's lives. It's easy to feel slighted when plans change or communication falters, but true understanding lies in recognizing that everyone moves at their own pace, guided by circumstances often beyond their control.

I thanked her for reaching out despite the distance, reassured by her voice that our bond remained steadfast despite the physical miles between us. We laughed briefly about the unpredictability of life and promised to catch up properly when she returned.

As I set my phone back down on the table, I couldn't help but feel a sense of gratitude. Most of all, gratitude for the reminder that true companionship isn't measured by constant presence but by the understanding and support that endure through life's twists and turns.

So she went, and I stayed, embracing the ebb and flow of life's journey with a newfound appreciation for the moments we share, whenever and wherever they may find us.

CHAPTER TWO

AUGUST

1stAugust

Truth is no one is here for you

We live in an era where virtual likes and comments can mimic support, where digital messages can give the illusion of companionship. Yet, when the chips are down and the night grows long, how many can you truly count on to be there?

It's not that people don't care. Many do. They express concern, they send good wishes, they click 'like' on your latest update. But when the silence falls, when the troubles weigh heavy on your shoulders, where are they then?

We're all navigating our own paths, carrying our own burdens, chasing our own dreams. It's easy to get caught up in the whirlwind of our own lives, to lose sight of those who may need us just as much as we need them.

And yet, amidst this realization, there's a flicker of hope. Because while no one may be here for you in the way you imagined, there are those rare souls who will show up when it matters most. They may not always know the right words to say or the perfect actions to take, but they'll stand by your side, offering their presence as a beacon in the storm.

These are the ones who listen without judgment, who hold your hand through the darkest nights, who remind you that you are not alone. They may be few and far between, but their impact is profound.

Perhaps the truth is not that no one is here for you, but rather that the ones who truly matter are here in a way that transcends mere presence. They are here in spirit, in understanding, in unwavering support. They are here, not because they have to be, but because they choose to be.

So, hold on to those who show up for you, who stand by you when others fade into the background. Cherish the moments of connection, however fleeting or profound they may be. And remember, amidst the noise of life's hustle and bustle, that the truth is not always as stark as it seems. There are those who care deeply, who are here for you in ways that defy expectation and redefine what it means to be supported.

In the end, the truth is not that no one is here for you. The truth is that those who are, are treasures to be cherished, for they illuminate the path forward with their unwavering presence and heartfelt compassion.

2ndAugust

Don't let go the string of hope

I received her call unexpectedly, her voice tinged with despair and uncertainty. She had embarked on a business trip full of anticipation, only to find herself confronted with realities far harsher than she had imagined. The journey that was meant to be a step forward had become a stumbling block, leaving her morale shattered and tears streaming down her cheeks.

She: "I don't know what to do... Everything's gone wrong. I thought it would be different."

Her words hung heavy in the air, a stark contrast to the optimism that had propelled her towards this opportunity. In that moment, I could feel the weight of her disappointment, the burden of expectations unmet.

Me: "I'm here for you. Take a deep breath. Tell me what happened."

As she poured out her heart, recounting the setbacks and unforeseen challenges that had clouded her journey, I listened with a mix of empathy and admiration. Here she was, facing adversity head-on, her vulnerability a testament to the strength it takes to confront disappointment.

Me: "It's okay to feel this way. You're allowed to be upset. But remember, this setback doesn't define your journey. It's just a part of it."

In the midst of her tears, I urged her to hold on to the string of hope, no matter how frayed it seemed. Because hope isn't just a fleeting emotion; it's a lifeline that anchors us in turbulent waters, guiding us towards calmer shores.

We talked about resilience, about finding silver linings in unexpected places, about the lessons learned from moments of adversity. Slowly, her tears subsided, replaced by a quiet determination to navigate this setback with grace and perseverance.

She: "Thank you for being here. I don't know what I would do without you."

As we ended the call, I reflected on the fragility of hope and the strength found in its tenacity. In a world where uncertainties abound and challenges loom large, it's easy to lose sight of the light at the end of the tunnel. But as long as we hold on to hope, as long as we support each other through moments of darkness, we can weather any storm that comes our way.

3rdAugust

I want to feel my feet

He: Hey there, how have you been holding up lately?

She: Hey. Honestly, it's been a bit rough. I feel like I'm walking on shaky ground, like nothing is certain anymore.

He: I'm sorry to hear that. What's been going on?

She: It's just everything, really. Work feels unstable, my personal life is a mess, and I can't shake this feeling of uncertainty. I just want some stability, you know?

He: I understand. It sounds really tough. Sometimes life throws us curveballs that we're just not prepared for.

She: Exactly. I feel like I'm constantly on edge, waiting for the next thing to go wrong. I want to feel my feet again, to have some solid ground beneath me.

He: I hear you. Maybe it's time to take a step back and evaluate things. Is there anything specific that's been weighing on your mind?

She: It's hard to pinpoint one thing. It's more like this overwhelming sense of not knowing what's coming next. I want to make decisions with confidence, not second-guessing every step.

He: That makes sense. Uncertainty can be paralyzing. Have you thought about reaching out to someone for advice or support?

She: I have, actually. Talking to you helps. It's good to know I'm not alone in feeling like this.

He: You're definitely not alone. We all go through periods of uncertainty. Maybe focusing on what you can control and taking small steps forward could help.

She: I'll try that. It's just hard to see beyond the fog sometimes, you know?

He: Absolutely. But remember, fog eventually clears. And until then, I'm here to listen and support you however I can.

She: Thank you. That means a lot. I guess I just need to find my footing again.

He: You will, I'm sure of it. And in the meantime, lean on those who care about you. We'll figure this out together.

She: I appreciate that more than you know. Thanks for being there, even when things feel uncertain.

He: Anytime. That's what friends are for.

~

4th August

Being Vulnerable is fine

She: You know, I've been thinking lately... I've always found it hard to be vulnerable.

He: It's okay, being vulnerable is fine. What's been on your mind?

She: I feel like I always have to have it together, you know? Like I can't let anyone see when I'm struggling.

He: It's understandable to feel that way. But remember, showing vulnerability doesn't make you weak. It shows strength in acknowledging your feelings.

She: I guess. It's just hard to open up sometimes, especially when I feel like I should have everything figured out by now.

He: I get it. We all have our moments of doubt and uncertainty. It's okay not to have all the answers.

She: Thanks for saying that. Sometimes I worry that if I let my guard down, people will see me differently.

He: True friends will understand and support you, no matter what. Being vulnerable allows for deeper connections and understanding.

She: I hadn't thought of it that way. Maybe it's time I start being more open about how I really feel.

He: It's a journey, and it takes time. But remember, you don't have to go through it alone. I'm here for you.

She: Thank you. It means a lot to have someone to talk to about this.

He: Anytime. Being vulnerable is part of being human. It's what makes us real and helps us grow.

She: You're right. I'm going to try to embrace it more. Starting now.

He: That's the spirit. I'm proud of you for taking this step.

She: Thanks for believing in me.

He: Always.

5thAugust

Patience can be painful sometimes

He:[sipping his coffee, looking contemplative] You know, I've been thinking a lot lately about how patience can be such a challenge. Sometimes it feels like waiting is the hardest part of any journey.

She:[nodding, stirring her latte] I hear you. It's like when you're waiting for something important to happen, and every minute feels like an eternity. It's almost as if time slows down just to make it more excruciating.

He: Exactly! I mean, we all know that patience is supposed to be a virtue, but when you're in the middle of waiting for something that really matters, it can be agonizing. It's not just about waiting; it's about how much it tests your resolve and your emotional state.

She:[sighing] Absolutely. I remember when I was waiting to hear back about that job application. Every day felt like a rollercoaster of hope and despair. It was exhausting.

He:It's interesting how the mind can play tricks on us during those times. You start imagining every possible outcome, both good and bad, and it can make the waiting even more intense. The anticipation is both thrilling and tormenting.

She:And then there's the added pressure of trying to stay positive and not let your anxiety get the best of you. It's like you have to force yourself to believe that everything will work out, even when it feels like the odds are stacked against you.

He:[nodding] Exactly. It's a balancing act between staying hopeful and not letting the uncertainty consume you. Sometimes I wonder if patience would be easier if we knew for sure that things would turn out well.

She: Yeah, if we had a guarantee, it wouldn't be patience, would it? It would just be waiting. The uncertainty is what makes it so painful.

He:True. And yet, I think it's that very uncertainty that teaches us the most about ourselves. It's in those moments of waiting and struggling that we discover our inner strength and resilience.

She:[smiling thoughtfully] You know, maybe patience isn't just about waiting; it's about how we navigate through that waiting period. It's about finding a way to stay grounded and hopeful, even when everything feels up in the air.

He: That's a beautiful way to look at it. Patience isn't just a passive state; it's an active process of managing our emotions and expectations. It's about learning to handle the pain and uncertainty with grace.

She:[raising her coffee cup] Here's to patience—painful, but ultimately a teacher of perseverance and resilience.

He:[clinking his cup with a smile] Cheers to that. And to finding peace in the waiting, knowing that it's all part of the journey.

6thAugust

Maturity in friendship kills the charm

She: [sipping her cappuccino, looking thoughtful] Have you ever noticed how maturity in a friendship sometimes seems to kill the charm? It's like once you reach that level of deep understanding, the spontaneity and excitement just kind of fade away.

He: [nodding, stirring his espresso] I get what you mean. When a friendship matures, it often becomes more stable and predictable. It's comforting in a way, but it can also feel like it loses some of its original spark.

She: Exactly! I remember when we first met, everything felt so fresh and thrilling. There was this constant buzz of discovering new things about each other, and every hangout felt like an adventure. Now, it's more about routine and deeper conversations.

He: [smiling] Yeah, there was a certain magic to those early days. The excitement of getting to know someone new, the unpredictability—it's a different kind of joy. But maybe that's just part of the evolution of a friendship.

She: I suppose so. It's just that sometimes I miss the spontaneity we used to have. Now, when we hang out, it's often planned and structured. It's like the charm of unpredictability has been replaced by the comfort of predictability.

He: [sighing] It's true. But isn't there something valuable in that predictability too? It's a sign of a deep, enduring connection. Even if the charm evolves, there's still a lot to be said for the stability and trust that comes with a mature friendship.

She: That's a good point. The deep understanding we've developed over time does bring its own kind of comfort. It's just that sometimes I wonder if that comfort comes at the cost of the excitement and novelty.

He: Maybe it's about finding a balance. We can cherish the new and exciting moments while also appreciating the depth and reliability that comes with maturity. Perhaps the charm doesn't have to disappear; it just changes form.

She: [smiling] I like that. It's about adapting and finding new ways to keep the spark alive. Maybe it's not about losing the charm but about redefining what charm means in the context of a deeper, more mature friendship.

He: [nodding] Exactly. And who knows? Sometimes, the most profound connections can bring their own kind of magic. It might not be as spontaneous, but it's just as meaningful in its own way.

She: [raising her cup] Here's to finding new ways to embrace the charm in our evolving friendships. It's all part of the journey.

He: [clinking his cup with a smile] Cheers to that. To evolving friendships and the different kinds of magic they bring.

7thAugust

You don't have to be so hard on yourself

She: [stirring her tea, looking concerned] You know, I've been thinking about how tough you've been on yourself lately. It's like you're constantly pushing yourself to be perfect, and it's starting to show.

He: [sighing, taking a sip of his coffee] I know. I've been feeling like I'm not doing enough, not achieving enough. It's like this inner voice never lets up, always reminding me of what I haven't done.

She: [nodding sympathetically] I get that. It's so easy to fall into the trap of self-criticism. But you don't have to be so hard on yourself. You're doing a lot more than you give yourself credit for.

He: [looking down at his cup] It's just that I set these high standards for myself, and when I don't meet them, I feel like I'm failing. It's hard to see the progress when I'm focused on what's left to do.

She: I understand. But sometimes, being your own harshest critic can be counterproductive. It's important to recognize and celebrate your achievements, even the small ones. They all count.

He: [nodding slowly] Yeah, I suppose I don't always take the time to appreciate what I've accomplished. I'm so focused on pushing forward that I forget to look back and see how far I've come.

She: Exactly. It's not about lowering your standards or giving up on your goals. It's about finding a healthier balance. You can still strive for excellence while also being kind to yourself and acknowledging your efforts.

He: [smiling faintly] It's a good point. I guess I need to learn to be more compassionate with myself. It's just hard to shift that mindset after being so self-critical for so long.

She: It takes practice, for sure. But remember, you're human. You're allowed to make mistakes and have off days. What matters is that you're trying and growing, not that you're perfect.

He: [looking thoughtful] I'll try to keep that in mind. Maybe I need to remind myself that being kind to myself doesn't mean I'm not ambitious or driven. It just means I'm human.

She: [smiling warmly] That's the spirit. It's about finding a balance between striving for your goals and being gentle with yourself when things don't go as planned. You deserve to be proud of your efforts.

He: [raising his cup] Here's to being kinder to ourselves and recognizing our own worth. It's a journey, but one worth taking.

She: [clinking her cup with a smile] Cheers to that. To progress, self-compassion, and celebrating every step along the way.

8thAugust

I asked her, 'When did you cry last time?'

He: [taking a sip of his coffee, looking curious] I was talking to someone the other day, and I asked her, 'When did you cry last time?' It got me thinking about how we handle our emotions.

She: [raising an eyebrow] That's an interesting question. What did she say?

He: She paused for a moment and said it had been a while. She seemed almost surprised by the question. It made me wonder—when was the last time I cried? And why is it sometimes so hard to really connect with our emotions?

She: [nodding thoughtfully] It's true, we often don't think about the last time we cried until someone asks. I think we tend to push those emotions aside or bottle them up. We might not even realize how long it's been since we truly let ourselves feel.

He: Exactly. It's almost like crying is something we're supposed to outgrow or avoid, especially as adults. But I think there's something important about allowing ourselves to cry and release those feelings.

She: I agree. Crying can be a release and a way to process emotions that we might not even fully understand. It's a natural part of being human, yet we often try to hide it or push it away.

He: [sighing] Yeah, I remember a few times in the past when I really needed to cry but held back. There's this weird notion that being emotional is a sign of weakness, when in reality, it's a sign of being deeply human.

She: [smiling gently] It's funny how society can make us feel that way. But crying isn't a weakness; it's a form of strength. It's about being in touch with our feelings and allowing ourselves to be vulnerable.

He: [nodding] It's also about how we deal with those emotions. I think when we don't cry or express our feelings, they can build up and affect us in other ways—like stress or even physical health problems.

She: Exactly. And sometimes, crying can be a form of self-care. It's like letting the pressure out of a steam valve. It helps us heal and move forward.

He: [smiling] I guess it's important to be in tune with our emotions and not be afraid to let them out. It's a way of honoring our own experiences and what we're going through.

She: [raising her cup] Here's to being more honest with ourselves about our emotions. Whether it's crying or simply acknowledging what we're feeling, it's all part of taking care of ourselves.

He: [clinking his cup with a smile] Cheers to that. To embracing our emotions and giving ourselves permission to be vulnerable.

9thAugust

Flowers

He: [glancing around the coffee shop, noticing the small vase of daisies on the table] You know, I've been meaning to ask you—what's your take on flowers? I've been thinking about how they seem to have a way of making any space feel more alive.

She: [looking up from her laptop, surprised] Oh, flowers? That's an interesting topic. I've always found them fascinating. They really do have a way of brightening up a place, don't they?

He: [nodding, taking a sip of his cappuccino] Definitely. I've been enjoying the sight of the daisies here. They're simple but cheerful. It made me wonder about everyone's favorite flowers and why they hold special meanings for them.

She: [smiling] I've always had a soft spot for peonies. They remind me of spring and renewal. They're so full and vibrant. What about you?

He: [thinking for a moment] I'd say sunflowers. There's something about their bright, bold presence that just radiates positivity. They seem to have this natural ability to lift your spirits.

She: Sunflowers are a great choice. They do have that warm, sunny vibe. It's amazing how they follow the sunlight. It's like they're always looking for the bright side of things.

He: [grinning] Exactly! And peonies have that same effect in a different way. They're so lush and rich; they make you feel like you're surrounded by abundance. It's nice how flowers can do that.

She: They really do have a special kind of magic. It's interesting how something so delicate can have such a strong impact on our mood and environment.

He: And let's not forget how flowers can mark significant moments in our lives. They often carry a meaning, whether it's a gesture of love, sympathy, or celebration. It's like they speak their own silent language.

She: [nodding] Absolutely. And even if they're not given with a specific message in mind, their mere presence can be a simple, heartfelt gesture. It's almost like they add a touch of nature's beauty to our daily routines.

He: [smiling thoughtfully] That's a lovely way to put it. Flowers have a way of making ordinary moments a bit more special. They remind us to pause and appreciate the beauty around us.

She: [raising her cup] Here's to flowers—the simple, beautiful things that add color and joy to our lives, reminding us to enjoy the little moments.

He: [clinking his cup with a smile] Cheers to that. To the small bursts of beauty that make our days brighter and our hearts lighter.

10thAugust

Is it hard for trees to shed their own leaves?

She: [stirring her chai latte, looking thoughtful] I was reading something interesting the other day about trees and how they shed their leaves. Do you think it's hard for them to let go?

He: [nodding, taking a sip of his espresso] That's a fascinating question. I mean, on one hand, it seems like a natural part of their life cycle, but I wonder if there's a struggle involved in it. It's not like they can just drop their leaves at will; it's a gradual process.

She: Exactly! I imagine it's not as simple as just deciding to let go. The way trees shed leaves is so methodical, like they have to go through a whole process to prepare for it. The change of seasons probably affects them quite a bit.

He: [smiling] It's like they're going through their own version of a transformation, isn't it? They're not just losing their leaves; they're preparing for a new phase. I suppose there's a kind of beauty in the way they embrace change.

She: That's a lovely way to think about it. It's like they're letting go of something old to make way for something new, even if it means a period of dormancy. There's definitely a sense of resilience in that.

He: [nodding] I guess there's also a certain wisdom in it. Trees don't seem to resist the change; they adapt and use it as a time to conserve energy. It's almost like they know that shedding leaves is a necessary step in their life cycle.

She: Yes! And it makes me think about how we, as people, handle letting go of things in our lives. Sometimes, it's hard to release what we're holding on to, but maybe there's something we can learn from the way trees do it so gracefully.

He: [thoughtfully] That's a good point. We often struggle with change and letting go, but observing nature's processes might help us find more acceptance. Trees show us that letting go isn't the end; it's just a part of a bigger cycle.

She: [smiling] I like that perspective. It's comforting to think that even in nature, there's a rhythm to change and renewal. It might make it a bit easier for us to embrace our own transitions.

He: [raising his cup] Here's to finding inspiration in nature's cycles and learning to embrace change with the same grace and resilience as trees.

She: [clinking her cup with a smile] Cheers to that. To letting go when necessary and trusting that new growth will follow.

11thAugust

Back to Basics

She: [sipping her cappuccino, looking thoughtful] You know, lately I've been feeling like we could all use a bit of a reset. Sometimes, it feels like we get so caught up in the complexities of life that we forget the importance of going back to basics.

He: [nodding, stirring his espresso] I've been feeling that too. There's something refreshing about stripping away all the excess and focusing on what really matters. It's like clearing out the clutter to make room for what's essential.

She: Exactly! It's easy to get overwhelmed by all the modern conveniences and distractions. I think going back to basics can help us reconnect with simpler, more fulfilling aspects of life. It's almost like a mental declutter.

He: [smiling] That's a great way to put it. Sometimes, it's the simple things that bring the most joy and satisfaction. Like spending time in nature, enjoying a good book, or having a meaningful conversation.

She: Yes! And it's not just about personal life. I've noticed that in our work too. We get so caught up in technology and processes that we forget the core principles that drove our passions in the first place.

He: [nodding] True. Reconnecting with those core principles can be really grounding. It reminds us why we started in the first place and helps us stay focused on our true goals and values.

She: And it's not just about simplifying, either. Sometimes, going back to basics means revisiting the foundational skills or knowledge that we might have overlooked. It's about honing what we originally found valuable.

He: [thoughtfully] Absolutely. It's like going back to the roots of a project or a goal. It can give us new perspective and help us refine our approach. It's about reinforcing the fundamentals.

She: [smiling] I also think it can be incredibly liberating. When you're not weighed down by unnecessary complexity, you have more freedom to be creative and authentic. It's like removing the barriers that were in your way.

He: [raising his cup] Here's to embracing the simplicity of going back to basics. To finding clarity, joy, and fulfillment in the essentials and letting go of the unnecessary clutter.

She: [clinking her cup with a smile] Cheers to that. To rediscovering what truly matters and building from a place of simplicity and purpose.

12thAugust

Nothing

She: [glancing up from her menu, curious] Hey, what's on your mind? You've been staring out the window for a while.

He: [taking a sip of his coffee, looking distant] Oh, it's nothing.

She: [raising an eyebrow] Nothing? Really? You look like you're deep in thought.

He: [smiling faintly] Yeah, it's just nothing. But sometimes, "nothing" can be quite revealing.

She: [intrigued] How do you mean? It's hard to imagine that nothing could hold much significance.

He: [leaning back, thoughtful] Well, when I say "nothing," it's not like I'm blank or disengaged. It's more like I'm absorbing everything around me—the quiet, the moments, the space between thoughts.

She: [nodding slowly] I get that. It's like when you say "nothing," it's actually a space where everything else can settle. Sometimes, the most profound realizations come from those quiet moments.

He: Exactly. It's in that "nothing" where you start to notice the little things—the patterns, the details, the feelings you might not have noticed otherwise. It's like a canvas where all the colors can come into focus.

She: [smiling] That's a beautiful way to look at it. It's as if "nothing" is a container for all the subtle, often overlooked aspects of life. It's where everything gets a chance to breathe and reveal itself.

He: [thoughtfully] Yeah, it's like "nothing" can hold a universe of experiences and emotions. It's not empty; it's full of potential and quiet understanding.

She: I think you're right. Sometimes, when we're busy or distracted, we miss out on the richness of those quiet, "nothing" moments. They're where we can truly connect with ourselves and what's happening around us.

He: [nodding] It's in those moments of apparent emptiness that we can find clarity and depth. It's where we can reset and come back to what really matters.

She: [raising her cup] Here's to embracing the "nothing" and finding the richness in those quiet, often overlooked moments. To the spaces that hold everything we need to understand ourselves and our world.

He: [clinking his cup with a smile] Cheers to that. To the beauty of "nothing" and the everything it holds.

13thAugust

The art of silence

She: [stirring her tea, looking contemplative] You know, I've been thinking a lot about the art of silence lately. There's something so profound about the way silence can speak volumes without a single word.

He: [nodding, taking a sip of his espresso] I completely agree. Silence has this unique ability to convey emotion and meaning in a way that words sometimes can't. It's almost like a language of its own.

She: Exactly. It's fascinating how silence can be so powerful. Sometimes, just sitting in silence with someone can create a deeper connection than any conversation.

He: [smiling] It's true. There's a certain intimacy in shared silence. It's like you're both in the same space, experiencing the moment together, without needing to fill it with words.

She: And silence can also be a space for reflection. It gives us the chance to pause, think, and process our thoughts and feelings. It's like a break from the constant noise and distraction.

He: [nodding] Absolutely. Silence allows us to tune into our inner world. It's in those quiet moments that we often come to the most important realizations or insights.

She: And it's not always easy to embrace. In a world that's constantly buzzing with sound and activity, finding peace in silence can be challenging. But it's so worthwhile.

He: [thoughtfully] It's true. We're often uncomfortable with silence because we're used to filling every moment with noise or conversation. But learning to appreciate silence can be incredibly rewarding.

14thAugust

Just one and loyal is enough

She: [sipping her latte, watching people chat and laugh around them] You know, I've been thinking about relationships and how we often get caught up in the idea that we need multiple partners or experiences to be happy. But sometimes, just one loyal and trustworthy person is all you need.

He: [nodding, taking a sip of his espresso] That's a really good point. It's easy to get swept up in the notion that more is better, but finding that one person who truly understands and supports you can be more fulfilling than a thousand fleeting connections.

She: Exactly. When you have someone who is genuinely loyal and trustworthy, it's like you've found a rare gem. No matter how beautiful or enticing the world might be, that one person becomes your anchor, your home.

He: [smiling thoughtfully] It's true. There's something incredibly reassuring about knowing that you have someone who's completely committed to you. It's a sense of security and warmth that can't really be matched by anything else.

She: And it's not just about having someone by your side; it's about having someone who's there for you in the truest sense. Someone who stands by you through thick and thin, who you can rely on without question.

He: [nodding] That kind of loyalty is rare and precious. It's like finding a soulmate who makes the rest of the world fade into the background. You're content because you know you have the one person who truly matters.

She: [smiling] It's comforting to think that in a world full of distractions and superficial connections, having one loyal person can make all the difference. It's like you don't need anything more because you already have everything you need.

He: [raising his cup] Here's to that one special person. To the loyalty and trust that make our lives richer and more meaningful. It's amazing how one person can change everything.

She: [clinking her cup with a smile] Cheers to that. To finding and cherishing the one who makes everything else feel like a beautiful bonus rather than a necessity.

15thAugust

Forever?

She: [sipping her cappuccino, gazing out the window at the bustling street] You know, lately I've been reflecting on what really excites me about our friendship. It's the reason I look forward to meeting you every day. There's something so comforting and fulfilling about our routine.

He: [nodding, taking a sip of his espresso] I feel the same way. It's amazing how something as simple as our daily coffee dates has become such a significant part of my life. But I can't help but wonder sometimes—how long will this last? Will it be forever?

She: [frowning slightly, setting her cup down] It's a question that's been on my mind too. I think we both treasure this connection so much that the idea of it not lasting feels a bit daunting. What if life throws something at us that changes everything?

He: [leaning back, thoughtful] I get that. It's almost like the certainty of our daily meetings has become a bit of a comfort zone. And while that's great, it also raises the question of how we handle the possibility of change. Will we be able to adapt if things shift?

She: [nodding] Exactly. It's not just about the routine; it's about the underlying bond we've built. I guess there's a certain fear of the unknown, of drifting apart or having our lives take us in different directions. It makes you wonder about the future of such a cherished friendship.

He: [smiling softly] But at the same time, I think there's something reassuring in the way we've built this friendship. We've managed to stay close despite the ups and downs of life. That's got to count for something, right?

She: [smiling back] Absolutely. It's not like we haven't faced challenges before, but we've always found a way to navigate them together. I think the real key is how we approach these challenges and whether we continue to make an effort to stay connected.

He: [sipping his coffee thoughtfully] And it's not just about effort. It's also about the mutual respect and understanding we have. It's those qualities that make me believe that even if life changes, the core of our friendship can remain strong.

She: [smiling warmly] I agree. The way we communicate and support each other is crucial. Even if we face new circumstances or distances, the foundation we've built can help us weather those changes. It's about valuing each other and making the conscious choice to stay in each other's lives.

He: [nodding] It's also worth noting that our friendship isn't static. It's grown and evolved over time, and I think that adaptability is part of what makes it resilient. We've learned and changed together, and I hope that continues as we move forward.

She: [thoughtfully] I love that perspective. It's about growing together, not just maintaining the status quo. As long as we're open to change and willing to adapt, I believe our bond can withstand the test of time.

He: [smiling] And there's something beautiful in that, isn't there? The idea that our friendship can evolve and adapt, but still remain a central, cherished part of our lives. It makes the concept of forever feel more like a journey than a destination.

She: [nodding] Exactly. It's about embracing the journey, with all its uncertainties and possibilities. Even if we can't predict the future, we can focus on the present and continue to build on what we have.

He: [raising his cup] Here's to the journey of our friendship. To embracing the changes and challenges that come our way, and to the joy of sharing these moments together, no matter how long they last.

She: [clinking her cup with a smile] Cheers to that. To the certainty that our friendship means the world to us and to the hope that it will continue to thrive, whatever the future holds.

He: [looking content] And even if there are uncertainties ahead, I'm grateful for what we have now. There's something special about being present in each moment and savoring the connection we've built.

She: [gazing out the window again, smiling] And you know, it's those everyday moments—the laughter, the shared experiences, the simple conversations—that make it all worthwhile. They're what create the fabric of our friendship.

He: [nodding] Absolutely. It's the little things that add up and make our friendship so meaningful. And even if the future is unpredictable, I feel confident that as long as we keep cherishing these moments, we're on the right path.

She: [smiling warmly] I couldn't agree more. Here's to celebrating the present and looking forward to whatever comes next, knowing that we have something truly special.

He: [smiling back] Cheers to that. To the strength of our bond and to many more days of coffee, conversation, and companionship.

16thAugust

Making peace with everything

She: [stirring her cappuccino slowly, gazing out the window at the bustling street] You know, I've been thinking a lot about the concept of making peace with everything lately. It seems like such a profound yet challenging goal. What are your thoughts on it?

He: [nodding, taking a sip of his espresso] It's definitely a complex idea. Making peace with everything seems almost like an ideal state of being, doesn't it? The notion of finding calm and acceptance in every aspect of life is both appealing and daunting.

She: [smiling thoughtfully] It really is. I think the idea of making peace with everything means finding a way to accept and embrace the ups and downs, the good and the bad. It's about coming to terms with life as it is, rather than how we wish it to be.

He: [leaning back, looking contemplative] Exactly. It's about letting go of the constant need to control or fix things. Sometimes, we get so caught up in trying to change situations or people that we forget the importance of simply accepting them.

She: [nodding] And it's not just about acceptance, but also about finding a sense of contentment and calm amidst the chaos. It's about being at peace with the things we can't change and focusing on how we respond to them.

He: [smiling] I think you've hit the nail on the head. It's about our response to life's challenges and uncertainties. Making peace with everything doesn't mean resigning ourselves to fate; it means choosing how we navigate the journey.

She: [thoughtfully] Yes, it's a conscious choice. It's about finding balance and understanding that while we can't control everything, we can control our attitude and approach. It's about embracing the present moment and finding peace in it.

He: [sipping his coffee] And I think making peace with everything also involves forgiveness—both of ourselves and others. Holding onto grudges or regrets only weighs us down. Learning to forgive and let go is a crucial part of finding that inner peace.

She: [nodding] Absolutely. Forgiveness can be incredibly liberating. It's about freeing ourselves from the burden of negative emotions and allowing ourselves to move forward with a lighter heart.

He: [smiling] It's also about being kind to ourselves. We often judge ourselves harshly and carry the weight of our mistakes. Making peace with ourselves involves self-compassion and recognizing that we're all doing the best we can.

She: [smiling back] I agree. Self-compassion is key. It's important to acknowledge our imperfections and understand that it's okay to make mistakes. It's all part of the human experience.

He: [thoughtfully] And I think making peace with everything also involves embracing change. Life is constantly evolving, and resisting change can cause a lot of unnecessary stress. Accepting change as a natural part of life can help us find more peace.

She: [sipping her tea] That's a great point. Change can be unsettling, but it's often through change that we grow and learn the most. Embracing it rather than fighting it can make the process smoother and more fulfilling.

He: [nodding] And sometimes, making peace with everything means letting go of our attachment to outcomes. We often have specific expectations or desires about how things should turn out, but being open to different possibilities can lead to unexpected and positive outcomes.

She: [smiling] It's about being flexible and open-minded. Life doesn't always go according to plan, and learning to adapt can lead to a greater sense of peace. It's about enjoying the journey rather than fixating on the destination.

He: [raising his cup] Here's to making peace with everything. To accepting the things we can't change, embracing the things we can, and finding contentment in the present moment. To letting go and trusting that everything will unfold as it should.

She: [clinking her cup with a smile] Cheers to that. To finding balance and serenity in the midst of life's challenges. To forgiveness, self-compassion, and the beauty of embracing change.

He: [smiling] And to the journey of discovering peace within ourselves and our lives. It's a continual process, but one that's incredibly rewarding.

She: [nodding] Absolutely. Making peace with everything is a lifelong practice, but it's one that brings a deep sense of fulfillment and joy. Here's to continuing that practice and finding peace in every moment.

He: [smiling warmly] Cheers to that. To a peaceful and fulfilling journey, wherever it may lead us

17thAugust

What makes them possible?

She: [stirring her latte thoughtfully, gazing at the people milling about the coffee shop] You know, I've been thinking a lot about what really makes relationships work. It's fascinating how some people manage to build such strong and lasting connections, while others struggle. What do you think makes it all possible?

He: [nodding, taking a sip of his espresso] That's an interesting question. I think a lot of it comes down to adaptability and understanding. Relationships aren't always equal, and sometimes the dynamics shift. It's about finding a balance and adapting to each other's needs.

She: [smiling] Exactly. It's not about perfect equality. Sometimes one person might give 100% while the other gives 0%, and that's okay. It's about the understanding that relationships are fluid, and the balance can shift over time.

He: [thoughtfully] True. Relationships are dynamic and require flexibility. There are moments when one person might be going through a tough time and can't contribute as much. In those times, the other person steps up. It's about support and being there for each other when it matters most.

She: [nodding] Yes, and it's important to recognize that this isn't necessarily a bad thing. It's not always about keeping score or ensuring that everything is perfectly balanced. Sometimes, love means giving more when your partner needs it and being okay with them giving more when you need it.

He: [smiling] Absolutely. Love isn't about strict equality. It's about understanding and being willing to adapt. Even when the balance isn't perfect, it doesn't mean the relationship is any less meaningful or valuable.

She: [sipping her tea] And it's also about acceptance. Sometimes, we might love someone deeply, even if they don't reciprocate in the same way. That's part of what makes relationships complex. Loving someone doesn't always mean they'll love you back in the exact same way, and that's okay.

He: [nodding] Right. It's important to accept that love can be one-sided sometimes. It's about giving from the heart without expecting something in return. If you genuinely care about someone, your love doesn't depend on their level of reciprocation.

She: [smiling softly] Exactly. It's the act of loving that matters, not necessarily how that love is returned. In the end, it's the genuine connection and the willingness to be there for each other that make relationships work.

He: [thoughtfully] And let's not forget about growth. Relationships require personal growth and adaptation. Sometimes, we have to learn and evolve to meet each other's needs. It's a continuous process of understanding and adjustment.

She: [nodding] Yes, personal growth is a huge part of it. Being in a relationship often means confronting your own challenges and learning from them. It's about growing together and supporting each other's growth.

He: [smiling] I think the key is to approach relationships with an open heart and mind. It's about being willing to adapt, to give and take, and to understand that perfect equality is unrealistic. What matters is the effort and the love you put into it.

She: [sipping her drink] I agree. It's about the journey, not just the destination. Every relationship has its own rhythm and balance, and that's what makes it unique. Embracing the imperfections and the shifts in dynamics is part of what makes relationships rich and fulfilling.

He: [raising his cup] Here's to the beauty of relationships. To the adaptability, the understanding, and the love that makes them possible, even when the balance isn't perfect. To accepting that love isn't always reciprocated in the exact same way, but it's still valuable.

She: [clinking her cup with a smile] Cheers to that. To the imperfections and the growth, to the moments of giving and receiving, and to the journey of building meaningful connections with those we care about.

He: [smiling warmly] And here's to appreciating the unique dynamics of each relationship. To loving wholeheartedly, understanding the ebb and flow, and finding joy in the connections we build, no matter how unbalanced they might seem at times.

She: [nodding] Absolutely. It's the willingness to adapt and the depth of connection that truly make relationships possible. Here's to continuing to nurture those connections with love and acceptance.

He: [taking a final sip of his coffee] Here's to that. To the effort, the flexibility, and the genuine care that make relationships so special. And to the journey we embark on with those we hold dear.

18thAugust

Where are you?

He: [sipping his coffee and checking his phone]

Phone buzzes with an incoming call. He answers.

He: "Hey! I was just starting to wonder where you were. Are you on your way?"

She: [voice sounding apologetic] "Hey, I'm really sorry, but something came up at work, and I might not be able to make it today. I hate to cancel on you."

He: [pausing for a moment, then smiling softly] "Oh, no worries at all. I completely understand. Work can be unpredictable."

She: "Thanks for being understanding. I was really looking forward to catching up, but it seems like I might be stuck here for a while. Can we reschedule?"

He: [taking a thoughtful sip of his coffee] "Of course, we can definitely find another time. I was just looking forward to our chat today."

She: "I know, and I'm really sorry for the last-minute change. I hope we can find a time soon that works for both of us."

He: "Absolutely. No harm done. It actually got me thinking about our friendship and how we deal with these situations."

She: "Oh? What do you mean?"

He: [reflectively] "Well, it's moments like these that make me realize how understanding we are of each other's lives and responsibilities. It's a sign of the level of understanding and attachment we have. We both get that sometimes things come up."

She: "Yeah, I see what you mean. It's reassuring to know that we can be flexible with each other. Not everyone has that kind of understanding in their friendships."

He: "Exactly. It's easy to have expectations, but when we can accept that life doesn't always go as planned, it shows the strength of our connection."

She: "I completely agree. It's comforting to know that our friendship can handle these little bumps. It makes me appreciate it even more."

He: "Same here. It's moments like these that make me value the depth of our understanding. It's not just about meeting up; it's about the support and patience we have for each other."

She: "I'm really glad you feel that way. I'm sorry again for missing today, but I'm looking forward to our next catch-up. It'll be even better when we finally get to hang out."

He: "No problem at all. We'll make it happen soon. And in the meantime, just knowing that we can navigate these little disruptions makes me feel good about our friendship."

She: "Absolutely. Thanks for being so cool about this. I'll make sure to make it up to you next time."

He: "Sounds good. I'm sure we'll have a great time whenever we get together. Take care of that work, and I'll talk to you soon."

She: "Will do. Thanks again for being so understanding. Talk
soon!"

He: [ending the call, reflecting] "It's moments like these that
remind me of how meaningful and strong our friendship is. It's
not just about the times we meet, but about the understanding and
support we offer each other day-to-day."

He looks around the coffee shop with a contented smile, feeling
grateful for the bond he shares with his friend.

19thAugust

Autumn in the Rainy Season

She: [entering the coffee shop, scanning the room for a familiar face] There you are! [waves as she spots him in the corner] Hey!

He: [glances up from his mocha, his gaze slightly lingering on the street outside before focusing on her] Oh, hi! [gestures for her to join him] I was just lost in my own world. How's it going?

She: [sits down, noticing his introspective mood] It looks like you're deep in thought. What are you working on today?

He: [flips open a well-worn diary and slides it over] Actually, I've been writing a new poem. It's called "Autumn in the Rainy Season".

She: [takes the diary, her curiosity piqued as she reads the poem aloud]

When autumn's whisper meets the storm,
And monsoon's tempest wild and bold
Unleashes winds that twist and warm,
The leaves are swept from green to gold.

They tumble not with graceful ease,
But wrested from their branches high,
Both tender buds and ancient leaves
Spun downward through the darkened sky.

A chaotic force, unplanned, unseen,
Takes hold of all, both young and old,

In nature's harsh and sudden scene,
Where even new and fresh grow cold.

Such is the nature of our days,
Where storms can come with ruthless might,
And sweep us from our chosen ways,
With futures lost to sudden flight.

We cannot mend what winds have torn,
Nor map a course through mist and rain,
But in the quiet work each morn,
We find peace amidst the strain.

So let the tempest rage its course,
And leaves fall where they may,
In daily tasks, we find our source,
And greet the dawn of each new day.

She: [looks up, visibly moved] Wow, this is really powerful. You have such an incredible way of seeing things. It's like you've captured the very essence of how life can be—unexpected, chaotic, yet beautiful in its own way.

He: [nods, a humble smile on his face] Thanks. I guess I try to find meaning in the everyday and translate that into words. It's not always easy, but it feels rewarding.

She: [reflecting] I remember reading your Spring Season edition, especially the poem WIND. There was that line, "loud thunder, it seems like issues inside her are presenting on the sky"—that book was great. It was so evocative and made me think deeply about how internal struggles can mirror the external world.

He: [interested] Really? I'm glad that line resonated with you. I tried to capture the idea of how personal turmoil can be reflected in nature's grandeur.

She: [enthusiastically] Absolutely. Your ability to express complex emotions through such vivid imagery is remarkable. Each poem seemed to connect with something profound and universal.

He: [smiling] I'm really pleased to hear that. I always hope to touch on those universal experiences we all share.

She: [nodding] Your poems have this way of making the intangible feel tangible. They evoke strong feelings and reflections, often leaving me with goosebumps.

He: [with a modest shrug] I'm just grateful that my words can touch others. It's what keeps me writing.

She: [smiling warmly] Well, keep doing what you're doing. Your ability to find beauty and meaning in the ordinary is truly special.

He: [grateful] Thanks, that means a lot. I'll keep at it.

She: [raising her coffee cup] Here's to more poems that make us think, feel, and connect. Cheers to that!

He: [raising his cup in return] Cheers! To finding and sharing those moments of clarity and connection.

She: [clinking her cup with his] And to more of your beautiful words that help us see the world in a new light.

20thAugust

Why are you so phlegmatic?

She: [sipping his coffee] "You know, I've been meaning to ask you something that's been on my mind. Why are you always so phlegmatic? I've noticed you're incredibly calm and composed, no matter what's happening around you."

He: [raising an eyebrow and looking up with a hint of surprise] "Phlegmatic? That's quite an intriguing choice of words."Phlegmatic? Honestly, I'm not entirely sure what that means. I've heard the term before but never took the time to really understand it. Could you explain it to me?"

She: [smiling] "Oh, really? You're a writer, and you don't know what 'phlegmatic' means? I find that a bit surprising. But alright, let me break it down for you. The term 'phlegmatic' refers to someone who is consistently calm, unemotional, and not easily excited or disturbed. It's one of the four temperaments in ancient psychological theory."

He: [nodding thoughtfully] "That's interesting. I suppose I didn't connect the dots. Even as a writer, there are so many words I'm not familiar with. It's like diving into an ocean—just because you can dive in doesn't mean you know the entire ocean. Writing is always a learning process. You discover new words and concepts every day, even every second."

She: "That's a wonderful analogy. And you're right—learning never really stops. But back to being phlegmatic. It's not just about being calm under pressure. It also involves handling situations with a steady and measured approach. Remember that time we were organizing the charity event and everything seemed to go wrong? You stayed so composed, and it really helped the rest of us keep our cool."

He: [smiling] "Oh, I do remember that. It was chaotic, but I tried to maintain a level head. I didn't realize that might be a defining trait of being phlegmatic. What other qualities do you think are associated with being phlegmatic?"

She: "Well, beyond staying calm, being phlegmatic also means being reliable and patient. You're someone who's always there when needed, and you handle discussions and decisions with a great deal of patience. You don't let your emotions take over, which helps in balancing things out, especially in stressful situations."

He: [reflecting] "That's a fascinating perspective. I suppose my approach has always been to focus on finding solutions rather than dwelling on problems. I never thought of it as a particular temperament. It's intriguing how understanding such concepts can offer new insights into our own behaviors and how we interact with others."

She: "Exactly. It's not just about labeling traits but understanding how they shape our interactions and relationships. Your calm demeanor really has a calming effect on everyone around you. It's a strength that not everyone possesses, and it's something I genuinely appreciate in you."

He: "Thank you. It's reassuring to know that my tendency to stay composed is seen as a positive trait. Sometimes, I wonder if I should be more expressive, but maybe this approach works well in its own way."

She: "Definitely. There's value in being able to stay calm and think clearly, especially in high-pressure situations. And it's not about suppressing emotions; it's more about managing them effectively. It helps in creating a stable environment for those around you."

He: [sipping his coffee] "I appreciate you sharing that. It's always enlightening to learn new things, even about oneself. And it makes me value the dynamic of our friendship even more. We each bring different strengths to the table, which balances out well."

She: "I'm glad you think so. It's these conversations that make me appreciate our friendship even more. We both have our unique traits that complement each other. It's a reminder of how understanding each other's temperaments can enrich our interactions."

He: "Very true. It's fascinating how a simple term like 'phlegmatic' can lead to such a deep reflection on our traits and relationships. I'm looking forward to exploring more concepts like this in our future conversations."

She: "Me too. And remember, if you come across any other terms or ideas that intrigue you, just ask. There's always something new to learn, and discussing it can offer valuable insights."

He: "Absolutely. Here's to continuous learning and growing, both personally and in our friendships."

She: "Cheers to that! And here's to many more coffee shop discussions that help us uncover new aspects of ourselves and each other."

He: [smiling warmly] "Definitely. Thanks for the enlightening discussion. I'm already looking forward to our next chat."

She: "Same here. Talk soon!"

He: "Talk soon!"

~

21stAugust

Peaceful Sunsets

A quaint coffee shop with a warm, inviting ambiance. Soft jazz plays in the background, and the aroma of freshly brewed coffee fills the air. He was seated at a window table, gazing out at the street with a serene expression. His friend entered the café and noticed his peaceful demeanor.

She: [walking in and spotting him at the table] "Hey! I didn't expect to find you so lost in thought. You look like you're in a different world. What's on your mind?"

He: [looking up with a gentle smile] "Oh, hi there! I was just... reflecting on something really beautiful I experienced recently. I didn't realize I was so absorbed in it."

She: [sitting down across from him] "It must have been quite something. What's got you so deep in thought?"

He: [sighing contentedly] "Well, it was this incredible sunset I saw the other day. It was at the Tawi River bridge. You wouldn't believe how peaceful it was."

She: [intrigued] "The Tawi River bridge? What made it so special?"

He: "It was an unusual combination of elements. It was raining, but at the same time, the sun was setting in the west, casting a brilliant, warm light across the horizon. I'd never seen rain and sunset happening simultaneously like that before."

She: "That sounds breathtaking. I can imagine how such a scene would be quite moving. How did it make you feel?"

He: "It was profoundly peaceful. The rain was gently falling, creating this soft, rhythmic sound, while the sunset painted the sky with vibrant colors. It felt like the chaos of the rain was inversely proportional to the tranquility it brought me. Even though the weather was stormy, the beauty of the sunset somehow balanced it out."

She: "That's such a beautiful way to describe it. It's like finding calm in the midst of turmoil. Did the combination of rain and sunset make you reflect on anything in particular?"

He: "Absolutely. It made me think about how often we find peace in the most unexpected places. Sometimes, it's in the middle of a storm that we discover the most profound calm. The serenity of the sunset, contrasted with the rain, reminded me that even in the midst of chaos, there can be moments of great beauty and tranquility."

She: "That's a really profound insight. It's amazing how nature can provide such powerful reflections on our inner states. Do you think this experience has changed the way you view such moments?"

He: "Definitely. It reinforced the idea that peace isn't always about having perfect conditions. Sometimes, it's about finding the beauty in the imperfections and contradictions of life. The sunset and rain together showed me that serenity often comes from embracing the full spectrum of experiences."

She: "I love that perspective. It's a reminder that even when things seem chaotic or unsettled, there can still be moments of peace if we're open to seeing them. Did you take any pictures or capture the moment in any way?"

He: "I did try to take a few photos, but they don't quite capture the essence of what I felt. It's one of those moments that's more about the feeling than the image. Sometimes, the most meaningful experiences are the ones we carry within us, not necessarily the ones we can show to others."

She: "I completely understand. Some moments are meant to be felt rather than documented. I'm really glad you shared this with me. It's a lovely reminder of how small moments can have such a big impact."

He: "I'm glad you think so. It's nice to have someone to share these reflections with. It makes the experience even more meaningful."

She: "Definitely. And it's a great reminder that there's beauty everywhere, even in unexpected combinations like rain and sunsets. Thanks for sharing this with me."

He: "Anytime. I always enjoy our conversations, especially when they lead to such thoughtful reflections. Here's to finding peace and beauty in all the moments of our lives."

She: "Here's to that! And to many more conversations about the beautiful and unexpected."

He: [smiling warmly] "Absolutely. I'm looking forward to it."

She: "Me too. See you tomorrow!"

He: "See you tomorrow!"

22ndAugust

Powerful Waterfall

A cozy coffee shop with large windows letting in the soft afternoon sunlight. The atmosphere was relaxed, with a few other patrons quietly chatting or working. The author and his friend were seated at a corner table, each with a cup of coffee.

She: [taking a sip of her coffee and gazing thoughtfully out the window] "You know, I've been reflecting a lot on how life's downs can be just as impactful as its ups. It's fascinating how moments of downfall can shape us."

He: [nodding in agreement] "Absolutely. It's like observing the natural world. Even the calmest of rivers, when faced with a sudden drop, transforms dramatically into a powerful waterfall. The character it displays at that moment is immense and sometimes even overwhelming."

She: "That's a vivid analogy. The way a river or stream changes when it encounters a great dip is a powerful metaphor for how we handle life's sudden challenges. It's a testament to the strength and character revealed during such times."

He: "Exactly. The waterfall's force and grandeur in its fall are remarkable. It reminds us that even when life takes us to the edge or when we face significant setbacks, our true character and potential can emerge in those moments. There's something almost majestic about the way a waterfall embraces its fall."

She: "It's true. And just like the river cannot stop its descent, we can't always control the highs and lows that come our way. What matters is how we respond to them. Our reactions and the way we manage these experiences define us more than the events themselves."

He: "Precisely. It's about accepting that both the highs and lows are part of our journey. The key is to navigate through them with resilience. And after going through such events, what's important is how we move forward, carrying only the lessons learned and leaving the rest behind."

She: "That's a very empowering perspective. I often think about how we can either let our downfalls consume us or use them as stepping stones. The way we choose to approach and learn from these experiences determines their impact on our lives."

He: "Yes, and it's crucial to recognize that each downfall has the potential to teach us something valuable. Sometimes, the most profound growth happens when we're faced with challenges. It's about harnessing that energy and transforming it into something constructive for our future."

She: "I completely agree. It's like the waterfall doesn't just fall; it becomes a part of a larger system, contributing to the river below and creating new paths. Similarly, our experiences, no matter how turbulent, contribute to our personal growth and the paths we take moving forward."

He: "Beautifully put. And it's comforting to know that while we may not be able to control the falls we encounter, we do have control over how we respond and what we take away from them. Each experience, whether high or low, adds depth to our journey."

She: "Absolutely. It's all about perspective and how we choose to carry those experiences. Learning from them and integrating those lessons into our lives helps us build resilience and wisdom."

He: "Exactly. And it's conversations like this that help reinforce that understanding. Sharing these reflections with you makes me appreciate the process even more, and it helps me see the beauty in every aspect of life's journey."

She: "I feel the same way. It's wonderful to explore these ideas and gain new insights. It's a reminder that no matter how challenging life gets, there's always a way to grow and find meaning."

He: "Indeed. And I'm grateful for these moments of reflection with you. They provide clarity and a sense of purpose, reminding us of the strength we carry within."

She: "I'm glad you think so. Here's to continuing our journey with a positive outlook and making the most of every experience."

He: "Here's to that. And to many more conversations that inspire and enlighten us."

She: "Absolutely. See you tomorrow!"

He: "See you tomorrow!"

23rdAugust

Gold Cappuccino

A stylish coffee shop with modern decor and a relaxed ambiance. The author was seated at a table near the window, sipping a cup of gold cappuccino. His friend walked in and spoted him immediately.

She: [walking in and spotting the author] "Hey! I see you're alrcady here. What's that you're drinking? It looks exquisite!"

He: [smiling and gesturing to the cup] "Hey there! This is a gold cappuccino. I thought I'd try something a bit different today. The gold adds a touch of creaminess and a richer taste compared to the usual cappuccino."

She: [sitting down and eyeing the drink curiously] "Gold cappuccino? That sounds intriguing. What makes it so special?"

He: [joking] "Well, besides the obvious golden hue, it's actually the texture and flavor that sets it apart. The gold dust gives it a unique creaminess that you don't get with a regular cappuccino. You should definitely try it."

She: [grinning] Ha, Haah, Haaa, "Alright, I'm game. Let me have a taste and see if it lives up to the hype."

He: [handing over the cup] "Go ahead. I'm curious to hear what you think."

She: [taking a sip and her eyes lighting up] "Wow, this is amazing! The texture is so smooth and the flavor is richer. You were right—it's definitely better than a regular cappuccino."

He: [chuckling] "I told you. There's something quite luxurious about it. I figured if we're going to have coffee, why not make it a bit special?"

She: [smiling playfully] "Well, you've certainly raised the bar. Now I'm going to expect every coffee date to come with a side of gold."

He: "I'll do my best to keep up with these high standards. But I must say, you're making it hard for me to find an excuse to make our coffee dates less extravagant."

She: [laughing] "Oh, so now you're saying I'm the reason you're splurging on exquisite drinks?"

He: "Maybe just a little. Your company is definitely worth it. Besides, it's not every day I get to enjoy such charming company along with my coffee."

She: [blushing slightly] "Well, I'm flattered. And I must say, it's always nice to have a little bit of luxury when catching up."

He: "It's a treat for both of us, then. And speaking of treats, I'm curious—what's the latest adventure in your world of work?"

She: [checking her phone] "Ah, actually, that reminds me—I've got an urgent call coming in. I hate to cut this short, but duty calls."

He: [grinning] "I figured as much. You always seem to have the most exciting (and sometimes urgent) work."

She: "It's part of the job, I suppose. But I promise, next time we'll have more time to enjoy our coffee without interruptions."

He: "I'll hold you to that. And in the meantime, I'll make sure to keep our coffee dates interesting enough to compete with the gold cappuccino."

She: [standing up and smiling] "Deal. Thanks for the delightful coffee and the even better company. I'll catch you soon."

He: "Looking forward to it. Take care of that work, and I'll see you around."

She: "See you tomorrow!"

He: "See you tomorrow!"

24thAugust

Carelessness

She: [sitting down and noticing the author's contemplative expression] "Hey, you look deep in thought. What's on your mind?"

He: [looking up with a thoughtful expression] "Oh, hey. I was just thinking about the concept of carelessness and how it affects our lives. It's something that's been on my mind lately."

She: [curious] "Carelessness? That sounds intriguing. What brought that up?"

He: "I've been reflecting on how carelessness can manifest in different aspects of life. It's not just about being negligent in small tasks but also about how it can impact relationships and personal growth."

She: "That's an interesting perspective. I've noticed that carelessness can have various layers. For example, it might start with small things, like forgetting an appointment, but it can extend to bigger issues, like not being attentive to important aspects of life."

He: "Exactly. It often starts small but can snowball into something larger. It's fascinating—and sometimes frustrating—how a seemingly minor lapse in attention can lead to bigger consequences."

She: "It can definitely create ripples. For instance, when someone is careless about their commitments, it affects not only their own life but also those around them. It can strain relationships and impact trust.”

He: “That’s a good point. I think carelessness often stems from a lack of mindfulness or awareness. When people aren’t fully present, they’re more likely to overlook important details or disregard responsibilities.”

She: “True. And sometimes, carelessness can be a result of feeling overwhelmed or stressed. When we’re juggling too many things, we might become careless as a way of coping with the pressure.”

He: “Absolutely. It’s like we’re trying to manage so many things at once that we lose focus on what’s really important. It’s a bit like trying to juggle too many balls and letting a few drop.”

She: “That’s a great analogy. It makes me think about how important it is to find balance and prioritize. Being aware of our limits and managing our time and energy can help reduce carelessness.”

He: “Yes, finding that balance is crucial. It’s about being intentional and conscious in our actions. When we take the time to be mindful, we’re less likely to overlook important details or neglect our responsibilities.”

She: “And it’s not just about being mindful for ourselves but also about being considerate of others. Carelessness can affect how we interact with the people in our lives, and being attentive can improve our relationships.”

He: “Exactly. It’s about creating a sense of trust and reliability. When we’re attentive and responsible, we build stronger connections and show that we value others’ time and efforts.”

She: "I agree. And sometimes, it's helpful to address carelessness directly. Talking openly about expectations and being clear about our responsibilities can help mitigate misunderstandings and prevent issues from arising."

He: "Definitely. Clear communication and setting boundaries are key. It's about creating an environment where carelessness is less likely to occur because everyone is on the same page."

She: "That makes a lot of sense. And I think it's important to remember that everyone can be careless at times. It's part of being human. What matters is how we address and learn from those moments."

He: "Absolutely. Acknowledging carelessness and making an effort to improve shows growth and maturity. It's about being proactive and striving to be more mindful in our actions."

She: "Well said. It's a continuous process of learning and adapting. And having conversations like this helps us reflect and refine our approach to life and relationships."

He: "I couldn't agree more. It's these reflections that help us grow and become more aware. Thanks for engaging in this conversation with me. It's been enlightening."

She: "I've enjoyed it too. It's always good to discuss these topics and gain new perspectives. I'll keep these thoughts in mind as I move forward."

He: "I'm glad to hear that. And I'm looking forward to our next chat. It's always great to catch up and share these reflections."

She: [standing up and checking her watch] "Actually, I have to run—another work commitment I can't miss. But let's plan to continue this conversation soon."

He: "Absolutely. See you soon!"

She: "See you tomorrow!"

He: "See you tomorrow!"

25thAugust

End of the day

As I sit here, sipping my coffee and watching the light outside gradually fade, I can't help but think about the end of the day. There's something oddly soothing about this time, a natural pause that invites reflection on everything that's happened. The world is winding down, and I find a quiet comfort in the transition from the busyness of daylight to the calm of evening.

It's a bit like how every story eventually comes to an end. No matter how complex or simple, every narrative has its final chapter. Whether it's a book, a film, or even our daily lives, that last scene is always present. I find it fascinating how endings bring both closure and the potential for new beginnings.

I often ponder how we approach these endings. Some stories conclude on a high note, leaving us satisfied and with a sense of resolution. Others end with lingering questions or a feeling of longing. It reminds me that not all conclusions are neatly wrapped up, and sometimes we have to find our own meaning in the ending.

Today felt like a whirlwind, filled with tasks, conversations, and moments that seemed to pass in a blur. But now, as the day draws to a close, there's a stillness that offers a chance to reflect. It's a moment to look back on the journey, to appreciate what has happened, even if it wasn't perfect.

I glance at my phone and realize that my friend won't be joining me today, caught up with work. There's a bit of loneliness in that, but I understand. Sometimes, we experience the endings on our own before moving forward. In these quiet moments, I can truly think about the meaning of the day and how I might approach the new beginnings ahead.

The café around me is winding down, and I observe the few remaining patrons and the soft ambiance of the evening. There's a certain beauty in the transition from day to night, from activity to rest. It's a gentle reminder that every ending also offers a chance to start anew, to regroup and prepare for what comes next. Each ending sets the stage for the beginning of another chapter.

As I prepare to leave, I carry with me the thoughts of today's end. It's all part of the larger story of life. Every ending, every close of the day, is an opportunity to pause, appreciate, and get ready for the next chapter.

These moments alone are valuable. They give me space to think, to reflect, and to be ready for whatever comes next. So, as I head out, I'm comforted by the idea that tomorrow will bring new possibilities. See you then, whenever our paths cross again.

26thAugust

Life is not easy, There must be some motivation that drives humans

As I sit here, staring into the depths of my coffee cup, my mind drifts to the notion that life is not easy. It's a thought that's been lingering in my mind lately—the relentless challenges and adversities we face. This world can often seem harsh and unforgiving, yet people persist and strive to find meaning despite the struggles.

Why is it that we continue to push forward even when the path is fraught with obstacles? What is it that drives us to live in a world that can sometimes feel so cruel?

I think about the myriad of reasons that motivate us. For some, it's the search for happiness or fulfillment. Even amid hardship, the pursuit of joy and contentment provides a reason to keep going. There's a deep-seated desire to experience life's pleasures, to find moments of peace and happiness that make the struggle worthwhile.

Then there's the pursuit of purpose. Many of us are driven by a sense of duty or a calling, whether it's to achieve personal goals, contribute to society, or make a difference in the lives of others. This sense of purpose can act as a beacon, guiding us through the darkest times and giving us a reason to endure the difficulties.

Relationships also play a crucial role. The bonds we form with family, friends, and loved ones offer us support and connection. In the face of adversity, these relationships can provide the strength and motivation we need to persevere. The love and care we receive from others, and the ability to give it in return, create a powerful force that helps us navigate life's challenges.

Moreover, there's a certain resilience within the human spirit. It's remarkable how individuals can adapt and overcome even the most daunting obstacles. This resilience is often fueled by hope—the belief that things can get better, that change is possible, and that our efforts will eventually lead to a more fulfilling existence.

As I reflect on this, I realize that life's difficulties are part of the larger tapestry of our existence. They shape us, teach us, and ultimately contribute to our growth. Each challenge we face adds depth to our character and strengthens our resolve.

So, despite the harshness of the world, there is an intrinsic motivation that drives us. It's found in the pursuit of happiness, the quest for purpose, the strength of relationships, and the resilience of the human spirit. These factors combine to propel us forward, even when life seems unforgiving.

In the end, it's this complex interplay of motivations that helps us navigate the difficulties of life. It's a reminder that while life may not be easy, the reasons to keep moving forward are deeply ingrained in our desires, connections, and inner strength.

As I finish my coffee and prepare to leave, I'm comforted by the understanding that these motivations are what make life worth living, despite its inherent challenges.

27thAugust

Coffee shop Changed

As I stand here, waiting for my coffee, I can't help but reflect on the recent changes. This café is different from the one where we used to meet—where she and I would sit for hours, discussing our days, sharing stories, and finding solace in each other's company. That place had become a cherished spot, a small sanctuary where our conversations flowed effortlessly.

But now, with her caught up in her work and unable to join me as she once did, things have shifted. The café, which was once a backdrop to our shared moments, feels different without her presence. The familiar routine of meeting here, of finding comfort in our conversations, has been interrupted.

So, I've come to this new café. It's vibrant, with a different energy—perhaps a bit too lively for my current mood. The clamor of voices and the rush of people serve as a stark contrast to the quiet, intimate atmosphere of the old café. I realize now that it's not just the coffee or the environment that made the old café special; it was the connection, the shared time, and the presence of a dear friend.

As I collect my coffee and prepare to leave, I'm struck by a sense of transition. It's more than just a change of place; it symbolizes a shift in our routines and the evolving nature of our friendship. Life's demands have pulled us in different directions, and while the essence of our bond remains, the settings and moments have altered.

It's a reminder of how transient things can be. Even the places where we find comfort and connection can change with time. The familiar can give way to the new, and we must adapt and find new ways to navigate these shifts. It's not about clinging to the past but embracing the changes and finding meaning in them.

As I step out of the café, clutching my coffee, I think about how life moves forward, whether we're ready for it or not. Our routines and the places we hold dear may change, but the essence of our connections and the memories we create persist.

In a way, this new café represents a new chapter. It's an opportunity to redefine my routines, to find new moments of reflection and connection, even if they're different from what I once knew.

With each step I take away from this place, I'm reminded that while change is inevitable, it's also an opportunity for growth. The essence of our friendship, the memories of those conversations, will always be with me, even as I move on to new spaces and new experiences.

So, I embrace this change, acknowledging the bittersweet nature of transition. Life's ebb and flow bring new opportunities and challenges, and it's up to us to navigate them with grace and openness.

28thAugust

On my own

As I sit here, enveloped in the familiar quiet of my apartment, I can't help but reflect on the solitude that now surrounds me. It's a solitude I know well—a space that once felt like a comfortable haven but now seems more pronounced, more palpable in the absence of her presence.

She used to be a constant in my routine, a regular companion whose visits and conversations filled the gaps of my days. We would meet often, sharing stories, laughing, and finding solace in each other's company. Her presence was a steady rhythm in my life, a reminder that even in solitude, connection was just a meeting away.

But now, she has moved to Bangalore for work, and I find myself once again on my own. The transition from having a close friend nearby to being alone again is more profound than I anticipated. The empty space where we used to sit and talk feels more expansive, a stark reminder of her absence.

There's a certain gravity to being alone, a reflection of the self that's often overshadowed by the noise of social interactions. It's in these moments of solitude that I'm faced with the raw reality of my own thoughts and feelings. The comfort of shared experiences has given way to a space where I must navigate my own emotions and find meaning in my own company.

Living alone is not new to me. I've spent many periods in solitude, finding solace in my own reflections and routines. Yet, the presence of a friend can transform the solitude into something more dynamic, more engaging. It's a reminder of how connections, even in their regularity, can profoundly impact our sense of belonging and purpose.

Now, as I settle back into the rhythm of being on my own, I'm reminded of the resilience that solitude can foster. It's a space where self-reflection becomes more acute, where the inner dialogue takes center stage. It's both a challenge and an opportunity—to rediscover oneself, to find new ways to fill the silence, and to embrace the freedom that comes with solitude.

I think about the future and how this period of being alone might shape my path. There's an inevitability to change, and with it comes the chance to explore new dimensions of oneself. The absence of her presence has opened a space for new experiences, new reflections, and perhaps even new connections.

So, as I sit here, alone but not entirely adrift, I embrace this time with a sense of acceptance and openness. Being on my own once again is a reminder of the ebb and flow of life—how people come and go, how routines shift, and how solitude can be both a challenge and a gift.

In this quiet, I find a space to reconnect with myself, to explore what it means to be alone, and to prepare for the new chapters that lie ahead. The absence of her is felt deeply, but it also serves as a reminder of the strength found in solitude and the possibilities it brings.

29thAugust

Passing Shower

As I sit here, listening to the rhythmic patter of the passing shower against my window, I'm enveloped in a sense of calm and introspection. The rain, so sudden and transient, brings with it a sense of fleeting beauty—a reminder of how quickly things can change.

The shower starts out as a gentle drizzle, a soft murmur that gradually intensifies, filling the air with its presence. It feels as though the world is momentarily transformed, wrapped in a cloak of rain and renewal. But just as quickly as it arrives, it begins to fade, leaving behind a sense of serenity and a quiet reminder of its brief visit.

In this moment, I find a parallel in my own life. Her presence, like this passing shower, was once a vivid and comforting part of my routine. When she was here, it felt as though I had a constant companion—a friend with whom I could share thoughts, discuss the highs and lows, and find solace in conversation. Her visits brought a sense of connection and hope, a respite from the solitary moments.

Yet, just as the shower passes, so did her presence. She came into my life like a refreshing rainstorm—offering hope, joy, and a reprieve from solitude. But as time moved on, her presence became less frequent, and eventually, she was gone. It's a poignant realization that the moments we share with others, while deeply meaningful, are often transient.

Her departure leaves a quiet space where her presence once was, much like the lingering calm after a rain shower. There's a beauty in how the rain refreshes the earth and then moves on, leaving behind a renewed landscape. Similarly, her time in my life brought a sense of renewal and hope, but as reality set in, her presence was no longer there.

As the last drops of rain fall and the clouds begin to part, I am left with a sense of acceptance. The passing shower serves as a metaphor for the nature of connections and moments in our lives. They come and go, sometimes leaving us in contemplation of their impact and their sudden absence.

This solitude, now that the rain has subsided, is a space for reflection and growth. It's a reminder that while connections may be fleeting, they bring with them moments of clarity and hope. The beauty of these transient moments lies in their ability to remind us of the depth of our experiences and the strength found in acceptance.

So, as I watch the remnants of the passing shower dissolve into the evening light, I embrace the impermanence of presence and the lessons it brings. The brief, beautiful moments of connection—like the rain—are cherished for their impact, even as we learn to move forward and find new paths in the quiet that follows.

30thAugust

Last Call

The author's quiet apartment in the evening. The phone rings, and he answers, finding her on the other end. Their conversation, filled with nostalgia and warmth, stretches into an extended, heartfelt discussion.

He: [Answering the phone] "Hello?"

She: [Voice tinged with a mix of excitement and sadness] "Hey, it's me. Do you have a moment to talk?"

He: "Of course! I was actually just thinking about you. What's up?"

She: "I have some news. I'm moving to Bangalore in a couple of days. It's happening so fast, and I just wanted to let you know."

He: [Surprised] "Wow, Bangalore? That's a big move. I wasn't expecting this at all. How are you feeling about it?"

She: "It's a mix of emotions, really. I'm excited about the new opportunities, but I'm also feeling a bit sad about leaving here. You've been such an important part of my daily life. I'm going to miss our conversations."

He: "I'll miss them too. We've shared so many moments and talks that meant a lot to me. It's hard to imagine not having those regular catch-ups."

She: "I know. It feels like we've been in this routine forever, and now everything is changing. It's a bit overwhelming."

He: "Change is always challenging. But maybe we can make the most of the time we have before you go. Do you think we'll be able to meet up before you leave?"

She: "I wish we could. But with everything that needs to be packed and arranged, I'm not sure if I'll have the time. But we can definitely have one last call, right? I want to make sure we have a proper goodbye."

He: "Absolutely. Let's make this call count then. Tell me about everything—how you're feeling, what's been going on. I want to hear it all."

She: "Well, it's been a whirlwind. I've been busy with work, trying to wrap up projects and prepare for the move. And there's just so much to do—finding a place, setting things up. It feels like there's always something new to tackle."

He: "I can imagine. Moving is such a big task. But think of it as an adventure—a new chapter with new experiences. Have you had a chance to explore Bangalore a bit?"

She: "Not yet. I'm planning to visit soon to look for a place. I'm hoping to find a nice spot that feels like home. It's strange thinking about starting over in a new city."

He: "It is strange, but also exciting. Every new place has its own character and charm. I'm sure you'll find a spot that you'll love. And we'll definitely have to plan a visit. Bangalore is a city with so much to offer."

She: "That's true. I'm looking forward to discovering it. But right now, I'm just focusing on getting everything sorted. It's been a bit of a juggle."

He: "I understand. Just remember to take care of yourself amidst all the chaos. Moving can be exhausting, both physically and emotionally. Make sure you get some downtime too."

She: "I will. Thanks for that. It's good to know you're thinking of me. Your support means a lot, especially during this transition."

He: "Of course. It's what friends are for. Even though we won't be seeing each other as often, I know we'll stay connected. We've built a strong bond, and that doesn't just disappear with distance."

She: "Absolutely. I feel the same way. And we'll have to keep in touch regularly—calls, messages, maybe even video chats. We can make it work."

He: "Definitely. We'll find ways to bridge the distance. And who knows, maybe I'll come visit Bangalore soon. It would be great to explore the city and catch up in person."

She: "I'd love that. We'll make it happen. And in the meantime, let's keep sharing our updates and staying in touch. I'll be looking forward to hearing all about your life and sharing mine with you."

He: "Sounds like a plan. I'm really going to miss you, but I'm also excited for you and this new journey you're starting."

She: "Thank you. I'm going to miss you too. But I'm hopeful that this move will bring new opportunities and adventures for both of us."

He: "I'm sure it will. And who knows, maybe this change will lead to even more interesting conversations and stories to share."

She: "Absolutely. Here's to new beginnings and staying connected despite the distance. I'm glad we had this chance to talk."

He: "Me too. It's been great catching up. Let's make sure to keep this connection alive. I'll always be here to listen and support you."

She: "And I'll be here for you as well. Thanks for being such a great friend. I'll talk to you soon, okay?"

He: "Definitely. Take care of yourself, and good luck with the move. I'm looking forward to our next chat."

She: "Will do. Talk soon!"

He: [Ending the call, feeling a mix of nostalgia and hope] "It's hard to say goodbye, but I'm grateful for the time we've had. Here's to new chapters and staying connected no matter where we are."

31stAugust

Final Goodbye...

The cozy coffee shop, once their haven for shared memories, now feels like an autumn scene, marking the end of a chapter. The rain patters softly against the window, mirroring the tears they both struggle to hold back. As they sit at their usual table, savoring their last Gold Cappuccino together, the air is thick with bittersweet nostalgia.

She: [Sipping her Gold Cappuccino, her voice a mixture of sadness and gratitude] "It's hard to believe this is our last time here together."

He: "I know. This place has become such a part of our routine. I'm really going to miss these moments with you."

She: "Me too. But I want you to know how much I've appreciated your friendship, especially during those tough times. You've been my rock."

He: "I'm glad I could be there for you. Your strength and resilience have been truly inspiring. I'll miss our talks and the way you always made things better." But before I go, I have something for you." [he hands her a small, wrapped gift.]

She: [Opening the gift to find a beautifully bound book] "Oh, this is lovely. Thank you. What's the title?"

He: "It's called Aonaran: Spring Season: Just Begun. I thought it might be something you'd enjoy."

She: "It looks great. I'll definitely read it. Thank you for thinking of me."

He: "And I have one more thing for you." [he hands her a small box.]

She: [Opening the box to find a delicate bracelet and a handwritten letter] "This is beautiful. Thank you."

He: [Nods, holding back tears] "Read the letter when you're alone. I hope it expresses how much our friendship has meant to me."

She: [Smiling] "I will. And I want you to know that you've made a lasting impact on my life. I'll always cherish our time together."

He: "I'll cherish it too. It's been a wonderful journey."

As their time together at the coffee shop draws to a close, they share one last embrace. The hug is warm and heartfelt, a silent acknowledgment of the bond they've shared. Their eyes glisten with unshed tears, but they both remain composed, not wanting to break down in front of each other. The rain outside begins to fall more heavily as they separate, reflecting their emotional departure from this chapter of their lives.

He: [Softly] "Safe travels. I'll miss you."

She: [Holding back her emotions] "I'll miss you too. Thank you for everything."

He: "Take care."

She: "You too."

The coffee shop is now quiet as she finishes her coffee and prepares to leave. After saying their goodbyes, she walks away, carrying the memories of their time together with her.

At Her New Destination:

She arrives in Bangalore, settling into her new surroundings. In a quiet moment, she takes out the letter he wrote and begins to read.

The Letter:

"As I sit down to write this letter, I find myself reflecting on the countless conversations, shared laughter, and meaningful moments we've experienced together. It's difficult to put into words just how much your friendship has meant to me, especially as you prepare to embark on this new chapter in Bangalore.

From our first meeting to the countless hours we've spent talking about life, dreams, and everything in between, you have been a source of support, joy, and understanding. Your presence has been like a constant beacon in my life, a comforting presence that has helped me navigate through both the highs and lows. The news of your move is bittersweet. While I am excited for you and the new opportunities that await, I can't help but feel a pang of sadness knowing that our regular catch-ups will be fewer and far between.

You've always had a remarkable ability to bring light into any situation, and I will miss our conversations that stretched into the late hours, our shared jokes, and the simple pleasure of just being in each other's company. Your move to Bangalore marks the end of an era for us, but I want you to know how deeply grateful I am for the time we've spent together.

Change is often challenging, and though the distance may be significant, our friendship will remain strong. It's built on a foundation of trust, respect, and countless memories, and those are not bound by geography. I have no doubt that this new chapter will bring you incredible experiences and growth, and I am eager to hear about every adventure you embark upon.

As you settle into your new life, remember that you have a friend here who will always be cheering you on. Whether it's through phone calls, messages, or visits, we will continue to share our lives, our stories, and our support for one another. Distance may separate us physically, but it will not diminish the bond we share.

Thank you for being such a wonderful friend and for the countless ways you've enriched my life. I look forward to the new stories we'll create, even if they're from afar. Until then, take care, embrace the new opportunities, and know that you will always have a place in my heart.

Wishing you all the happiness, success, and fulfillment in this new journey."

Back to Basics:

As she starts her new life in Bangalore, he returns to his quieter, introverted routine. The energy and warmth of their recent interactions fade into a gentle nostalgia, but the impact of their friendship remains etched in his heart. The book Aonaran: Spring Season: Just Begun rests on his shelf, a reminder of the connection they shared and the new beginnings that both are now facing.

He reflects on the quote: *"If you love her, then you should let her go. If she comes back, then she's yours."* A small smile tugs at his lips as he contemplates the meaning, a question lingering in his eyes.

Autumn's Farewell

As Autumn's breath cools the air, where amber leaves descend,
The final hues of daylight dance, as day and twilight blend.
The café's warmth now feels more dear, as seasons softly wend,
To bid farewell to fleeting days, and watch the autumn end.
The golden cups of memories shared, now touched by autumn's
grace,
Echo laughter, soft and sweet, in this serene, familiar place.
The friend, who brought such light and cheer, now leaves without a
trace,
Her absence marks the season's change, as time quickens its pace.
The leaves that fell, so bright and bold, now blanket streets in gold,
Each whisper of the wind recalls the stories that were told.
The crisp air carries notes of change, as Autumn's tales unfold,
In every breeze, a sigh of thanks, in every leaf, a fold.
The warmth we shared, now memories, in the twilight's gentle
glow,
Marks the end of Autumn's reign, where new beginnings start to show.
The echoes of our final talks, in every sunset's throw,
Are etched in the heart's quiet space, where the softest feelings grow.
Autumn's farewell is not the end, but a shift in the season's song,
A gentle close to what we knew, where the echoes now belong.
In every leaf that drifts away, in every dusk's prolong,
There lies the hope of fresh beginnings, where the heart remains
strong.
As the last of Autumn's days retreat and winter's breath draws
near,
The warmth of shared moments lingers, even as we shift gears.
For in the farewell's quiet grace, and the memories we revere,
We find the beauty of transition, in each passing, golden year.